BLOOD AND BACK STITCHES

STITCHES IN CRIME
BOOK 7

ACF BOOKENS

1

The ranunculus had been pushing up through the last vestiges of snow and ice for about two weeks now, and as these early spring days warmed I was thrilled to see their purple and pink buds starting to swell. They were some of the first flowers of spring, if you didn't count the tulip bulbs that were still sitting in my laundry room unplanted, and I was ready for them.

Winter had been long here in Octonia, with more snow than usual and a lot of rain. Snow was fun for both Sawyer, my almost four-year-old son, and me for about fifteen minutes, and then we were both over it. We did differ, however, in our affection for mud – he was a huge fan, and I didn't love using my mop that much.

But it wasn't just the fact that I could comfortably hose my child off now that the temperatures were beginning to warm that made me grateful to see the flowers. I was also very glad to be able to get back to salvaging buildings. We'd taken a couple of months off for the holidays and the worst of the cold weather because I didn't want to put my friend Saul or his crew through the intensity of working in the frigid air. But now with temperatures in the fifties and some sun to dry up at least a little of the mud, we had our first salvage job of the season.

When adding the fact that Sawyer was beginning preschool for the first time this week, I was practically jumping out of bed on a Monday morning. I would have made it upright much more quickly if there hadn't been a young child clinging to my neck and trying to tickle me, but I couldn't resist a little tickle fight with my big guy.

"Stop it, Mama," he shouted through his giggles when I tickled him back, and I did what he asked.

"Had enough, Love Bug?" I said as I put my feet on the floor and stretched. Someday this little guy was going to want to sleep in his own bed next door, but until that day came, I was content to let him sleep with me even though it meant I had his feet in my lower back all night.

"Let's go," he shouted as he wiggled over to my side of the bed and dropped to the floor. "I'm ready to get dressed."

For a moment, I just stared at him as he headed to his room to – presumably – find some clothes. Saw *never* wanted to get dressed, but apparently, the tide of nervousness about school had swelled into a wave of excitement instead. I was on board with that, and as I slipped a sweatshirt over my own head, I heard the drawers of his dresser opening and closing. There was no telling what he was going to be wearing, but as long as it was clothes, I didn't care. Better he announce his strong personality from day one than to have me temper it.

A few moments later, he returned to my room and did a spin, a la Jonathan Van Ness, and said, "How do I look?"

I smiled. "You look amazing, Wild Child. Lots of our favorite color. I love it." I grinned as I studied his blue jeans, his blue T-shirt, and his blue Captain America cape and mask. "Great choice for your first day."

"I'm Captain America," he said as he put his arms up and over his head and "flew" down the stairs.

On a whim, I grabbed his Wolverine mask and cape, donned them, and charged down the stairs after him. "I'm going to win," I said. "Beat you to the kitchen."

It was just growing light outside, but the sky was a brilliant gold as Saw and I tore through the living room into the kitchen. He won, as always, and not because I let him, and when he dropped right into his chair at the table and said, "Oatmeal, please," I could only stare. In addition to never wanting to get dressed, he also never wanted to eat. Clearly preschool was a game changer in a lot of ways.

Fortunately, it did not change my little guy's desire to help me cook, so he quickly went from sitting in his chair to dragging it over to the stove, where we boiled water, added the oats, and watched carefully as it thickened up. A few raisins, a little milk, and a teaspoon of honey finished off our breakfast, and we sat down to eat and talk about school.

A few minutes later, I was dressed, Saw was in his car seat, and Beauregard, our Maine Coon cat, was seated on the front seat next to me after refusing to be left behind. He appeared to be as excited as I was to see how Sawyer took to school. On the short drive there, Sawyer grew more quiet, and I watched him carefully in the rearview mirror.

My son was like me, and new things were both a source of excitement and nervousness for him; but I'd learned that the way he wanted to handle those feelings was to sit with them, unlike his mother who had spent most of her life avoiding her negative emotions. So I stayed quiet as he dealt with how he felt, and by the time we got to the small preschool near where his father worked, he was all smiles again.

As I took Saw out of his car seat, I saw his father walking across the parking lot. Neither of us wanted to miss Saw's first day of school. The three of us opened the front door and walked in together, and Sawyer clung to my leg for a minute until a woman with pigtails and a huge smile asked him if he wanted to play in the sand table with the little girl who was already there.

He looked up at me, smiled, and then took off, cape flying, toward the table. We watched for a couple of minutes as he played, and then I called, "Have a good morning, Love Bug! I'll see you in a few hours."

As he grinned and waved to his dad and me, I felt the tears prick my eyes and quickly turned to go. He was going to be fine, and so was I. I needed to let myself feel my feelings, too, but not in front of my ex. He didn't get that privilege anymore. I gave him a quick wave goodbye and walked to my car where I turned on the engine, drove out of the parking lot, then promptly pulled into a church lot a bit down the road so I could cry.

My sadness tended a few minutes later, I pulled back out on the road and headed toward the jobsite up in the mountains near the edge of the Shenandoah National Park. As I drove up the winding road, my excitement started to build. This was going to be my first antique log cabin job, and I was so eager to see what we could salvage from the two-hundred-year-old building.

A bit of online research had given me a little history of the building. It had been built by Irish immigrants, the O'Malleys, who had come over to the States at the beginning of the nineteenth century. They had been subsistence farmers for the first few decades, living off what food they could grow and what animals they could raise, but then the railroad had come through, and most of the men in the community went south to help build the tunnels that ran through the Blue Ridge.

It was a hard time, but the men who survived returned home with a bit more money and a lot more skills to support their families. The O'Malley family bought more acres of land, a bit down the mountain where the soil was more fertile and the terrain flatter, and they soon had a thriving business of growing feed corn and harvesting bark for the tanyards just over the closest ridge. Life was good for the O'Malleys.

But then, President Roosevelt built a hunting cabin nearby and fell in love with the Blue Ridge. Soon, he had plans for a national park, plans that included moving all the families off their land by declaring eminent domain. It was a bitter piece of Virginia history, one that had forced the O'Malleys off the mountain.

Technically, their land hadn't been part of the park proper, but the only roadway that now accessed their farm ran through what had been declared park land. Since the Park Service had closed all the smaller roads up the mountains to control access to the park, the O'Malleys then had to drive to the top of the ridge, come in through the park, and make their way down a logging road to their farm. It was a laborious process, I imagined, with only horse and wagon, and I could understand why the family soon abandoned their farmstead and moved closer to Octonia town.

When Frank O'Malley had contacted me about salvaging his family's cabin, I had immediately been interested, because of both the story and the wood. I had offered him more than a fair price for the logs, and when his only counter was that he wanted the hearthstone from the main room in the cabin if it was possible, we had quickly come to terms and drawn up a contract. Today was the day we were going to take the cabin down, and I at least hoped it would be as easy as coming to the terms.

Over the weekend, Saul and his crew had opened up an old logging road so that it was passable for "most vehicles except those tiny, silly ones," Saul had said. As I turned onto the road, I thought that in Saul's case the words *silly* and *tiny* applied to most vehicles since my Subaru Outback was barely making it up the road. *Thank goodness for all-wheel drive,* I thought.

The last few feet of driving were treacherous, with a hairpin turn and a sheer dropoff on one side, but when I parked by the old cabin and looked back at where I had come, I gasped. The view was spectacular, and I let myself both appreciate it and feel what must have been the profound sadness the O'Malleys must have felt when they had to abandon this place.

I could see almost to Richmond, it felt like, and as the Blue Ridge Mountains ended, I could see the Southwestern Mountains and then the flats of Louisa County that led all the way to the shore. It was breathtaking, and on a clear day like that one, it felt like the whole world lay at my feet. For a brief minute, I let myself dream of living up here, imagining evenings on the porch with the sun behind me and a warm drink in my hand.

Then I thought of the road, of the distance to Sawyer's school, and of my own wonderful farmhouse just down the mountain, and I let myself be grateful for the chance to be in this place and for the space I called home. It wasn't either/or. It was both. And more.

Saul let me gawk for a couple of minutes, but as usual, he was eager to get started and I didn't blame him. His forklift sat at the edge of the flat space around the cabin, and if he made a mistake in judging the space, he and that machine were going to take a long tumble down the hillside. I could see why he wanted to be done with this particular job. "You ready, Paisley-girl?" he said as I walked over to where he stood by his machine.

"As I'll ever be." I glanced back over my shoulder at the view one more time. "Any chance I can get you to take me up on those forks to see from up there?"

Saul grinned. "You know I'm always game for a daredevil mission, but let's save that as a treat for the end of the job, okay?" He eyed the building. "You been in yet?"

"Nope. You?"

He shook his head. "I'd like you to do the honors."

I smiled. "Thanks. Join me?" I held out my arm for him to take, and he slid his hand into the crook of my elbow.

"Lead the way."

As I walked through the door of the house, my breath caught for the second time that morning. I let Saul through the threshold, and then I turned back and pointed. The walls were at least twelve inches thick and made up of a single log on each tier. "These trees were massive," I said.

Saul ran a hand along the interior face of the square-cut log. "Virgin timber, I expect. Hewn from around here by the look of it." He leaned in and took a close look at the grain. "Oak. It was hard work to build this." He wrinkled his nose a little as he stood.

I nodded. Oak was heavy and dense, and as the marks in the logs attested, the work had been done by hand with axes and saws. The O'Malleys had been serious about staying put when they built this cabin. It was a work of art.

A bit more study, though, revealed that the cabin was succumbing to the elements. A couple of the top log tiers showed some rot, and I suspected that there was termite damage up near the roof, too. By and large, though, the logs were in great shape, and I was going to come out financially *way* ahead if we didn't find any major problems with the building as we began to disassemble it.

The structure was very simple in layout. A large front room included the huge stone fireplace, which was used for cooking and for heat, a kitchen full of knotty pine cabinets next to the chimney, and a cozy sitting area. At the back of the room, directly across from the front door, was the single bedroom where all the members of the family would have slept.

Frank O'Malley had told me they slept head to toe in the two beds, everyone together. I didn't mind sleeping with Sawyer, and once or twice now Santiago had stayed over when Saw was there, and the three of us could make it work in a queen with a toddler sandwiched between two adult bodies. But more than two adults in a bed was too many limbs for me to think about navigating in my sleep.

As I headed toward the door to the bedroom, I heard Saul behind me giving directions to the crew, who had been climbing on the roof and securing straps to begin the work. They were as eager as their boss to get moving, so I knew I was running short on time to scope out the interior.

The back room was as empty as the front one. All the furniture had long since been removed, and since this was a log cabin, there wasn't much on the interior anyway. Frank had been fastidious about taking everything out of the building for us since he felt it important that we not have to deal with any "junk" as he called it. I had actually been a little sad about that. Sometimes what people thought of as *junk* was really the great stuff.

When I saw the small pile of something in the back corner of the room, I thought of junk and great stuff and felt my heart pick up its pace a little. *Treasure*, I thought as I made my way over to the corner. As I got closer though, my steps slowed. Whatever was in that corner was long and thin and covered with what looked like a very modern black comforter. Given that no one had lived in this cabin for almost one hundred years, I didn't think it was likely that a polyester blanket was some forgotten family heirloom.

Behind me, I heard Saul walk in and as he stepped toward me, the smell hit. It was sweet, like rotting fruit, but also musty. On instinct, I leaned back, bumping into Saul in the process. I began to shake my head. "No. No. No," I whispered.

Saul put his hands on my shoulders. "Stay put," he said as he stepped around me. Very slowly, he lifted the corner of the blanket closest to us and the back wall of the cabin.

As the fabric rose, the smell bloomed and I gagged. I couldn't even take a deep breath to steady myself, but I forced resolve into my throat. There beneath the blanket was a man, a young man. A young white man. A dead young white man.

The fabric dropped from Saul's hand, and he said, "Crap." He folded his arms behind his head and walked a circle around the room. "I'll tell the guys to stop work."

I sighed. We'd unfortunately been in this situation way too many times, and we both knew the protocol. I also knew, given my undesired experience with finding human remains, that this man had not been dead long – a couple of days, maybe. My cabin project was now an active crime scene.

As soon as Santiago Shifflett, the sheriff, picked up the phone, he said, "I so hope you're calling to tell me, as your boyfriend, that you hit the mother lode with this cabin and we're going to take Sawyer on a safari. Please tell me this is a casual call, Paisley."

I felt terrible. My salvaging work had made his workload so much higher, but he had to know. "I'm afraid not," I said. "How soon can you get here?"

"See you in thirty," he said as the phone moved away from his ear. But then his voice got louder again. "You okay?"

"As okay as I can be. See you soon." I hung up and followed Saul back out of the building. Then, I climbed into my car and cried for the second time that day. This was becoming an unwelcome pattern. A very unwelcome one.

2

As I waited in my car for Santiago, I pondered the guilt I felt about finding all these murdered people. It wasn't my fault their bodies kept winding up in the buildings I was salvaging from; my rational mind knew that. But that poor man in the bedroom made six dead human beings that I had found, and it was beginning to feel personal.

I'd said as much to Mika and Santiago both, and both of them assured me that none of these terrible deaths were about me. "In fact," Mika had said the last time I brought up the topic, "maybe you should think about it like this: You are actually giving people peace and helping their families find some closure."

I had to admit she did have a point. I did find the experience of finding out the stories of these people to be really valuable to me, and not just for my business. I'd always understood people and the world through stories, and each time I delved into the lives of the people whose bodies I'd found, it was an honor.

Still, with that man's corpse resting inside my latest salvage project, I didn't feel so much honor as I did sadness and not a small amount of fear. Either the man had laid himself under that blanket and died quietly, or someone had put his body there. Neither scenario was pleasant to consider, and I didn't want to be the one who had to tell Frank O'Malley that there was a dead body in his family's antique cabin.

Fortunately, that job didn't fall to me, and as soon as Santiago's cruiser pulled up next to my car, I felt a little of the weight of the moment pass from my shoulders. I hated that it passed to him, this man I loved, but I knew he accepted the burden of his police work gladly. He was a true civil servant, and when it came to solving mysteries, he was relentless, especially when the mystery involved a dead body.

I stepped out of the car as he parked, and when he pulled me to his chest and held me close, I relaxed a little further. When I stepped back, he met my gaze. He didn't have to ask if I was okay anymore. He could just look at me, and I knew that was his first concern.

"I am glad you're here, Santi." I took his hand, and we walked toward the cabin.

I sighed. "Frank O'Malley seems like the kind of guy who would have at least given me a heads-up if he suspected anything untoward had been going on up here."

"I had the same impression." Santiago stopped at the door and shook Saul's hand. "If this doesn't look like the crime was committed here, we may be able to get you all back to work this afternoon."

I heard a car pull in and looked to see Savannah Wilson, Santiago's main deputy, step out of her car. She gave us a small wave and then began what I knew would be her careful perusal of the area around the cabin. Unfortunately, Saul and I were very familiar with this routine, so he'd already corralled his guys into one area so that Savannah could do her job. And I knew she'd ask the men where they'd walked and make a careful map of all the footprints she found. It wasn't likely her usual techniques would yield much here given how much mud surrounded the cabin and how much prep work Saul and his crew had done to make the area passable for cars, but if there was something to find, Savannah would find it.

"He's in the back room," I told Santiago, and then I watched him slip booties over his muddy boots and walk inside. Usually, he didn't take that level of precaution, especially when others had been in the house before him, but given the mud, I guess he thought it best to try and preserve any footprints on the boards inside.

I leaned against the side of the cabin and took in the view again. Despite my whimsical visions of living with Santiago and Sawyer up on a mountainside, I was really someone who took her strength from the base of the mountains. I loved looking up and seeing the gentle peaks of the Appalachians watching over me. They felt like a kind mother, a gentle woman looking down and lending me strength. I didn't know if I could give that up even to have this sort of outlook from above most of life.

My musings were interrupted when Santiago came to the door and said, "Just to be sure, neither of you knows that man, correct?"

"Nope," Saul said. I shook my head.

"Okay, the coroner is on his way, but I don't see any sign that he died here." Santiago shook his head. "It's going to be a long day."

I groaned. "So you think someone put his body here?"

"The coroner will confirm, but yeah. I'd guess he's been dead a week, maybe more." He swallowed hard. "Without getting into too much detail about how the process of decomposition works, I'll just say that I think he was probably moved here recently. Maybe even today."

"Today?!" Saul said. "So that someone would find him."

Santi nodded. "That's my guess." He turned to me. "Pais, I'm going to need to know the name of anyone who knew you were coming up here to start work today."

This time my groan came out as more of a roar. "I'll print out my email list. I told everyone about the project in my newsletter on Saturday."

Santi's face fell. I had just created a suspect list of over 1,000 people. The day couldn't really get much worse for him.

Fortunately, I was saved from contending with my own guilt for a little bit when Savannah walked into the cabin with a charcoal-gray sheet. "Found this out behind the house."

"Looks like it might match what the guy is covered in," Santi said and pointed toward the back room.

Savannah gave me a nod and then set her hand on my arm. "You okay?"

I sighed but then nodded. "Yeah." The two officers headed in and I went back to gazing at the view.

Saul leaned his shoulder against mine and said, "You know, you could just gather things from auctions and stuff if this is becoming too much."

I glanced at him out of the corner of my eye, and I appreciated that he was doing the thing men are trained to do: offer an idea but then look aloof about the response. Today, I needed that distance because his suggestion was pretty powerful. I had thought of it myself on a number of occasions, and today it was really, really appealing.

But even as I turned the idea of visiting auctions and picking up items that I could make enough of a margin on to pay my bills, I felt distaste for the idea rising up. Part of why I loved what I did was that I was rescuing things that no one else knew had value. If I didn't do this work, sure, someone else might step in and salvage these buildings and the bits and bobs of history that I gathered, but they might not either. Then, those things would be lost.

Even more, though, I wanted to be the one to save them. I wanted to find these treasures and get them into new homes. That was part of my role in this world, and I would be hard-pressed to give it up.

Finding dead bodies all the time was pressing pretty hard though, too. I let out a long sigh.

"I know that's not what you want to do, Paisley-girl," Saul said. "But know it's an option if you need one, okay?"

This time when I glanced over he was studying my face. I smiled as best I could and nodded. "Thanks, Saul."

Santi and Savannah walked out. "I'm going on a hike," Santi said. "Want to come?" He looked at me and waited.

"I'll stay here, wait for the coroner," Savannah said.

"Me, too," Saul said as he sat down on the step. "I just spotted a cedar waxwing." Saul was an avid bird watcher, but that wasn't something he told everyone. It didn't quite align with the rough, rugged persona he projected for most people. I knew he was a softy, though, and I also knew he was trying to give Santiago some time alone while also keeping Savannah company. Saul was a good man.

I followed Santi back the way Savannah had just come, and as we walked, I tried to get my nerves to settle. It would do no one any good if I was all jangly and awkward, and Santi didn't need to be worrying about me while he was trying to get the lay of the land about a murder. So I took deep breaths and attended to the tiny shades of green that I was beginning to see among the trees.

Finally, I asked, "What are we looking for?"

"I have no idea," Santi said as he stopped and looked around before taking my hand. "But given how pristine this place is, I think we'll see anything out of the ordinary."

"Got it," I said as I squeezed his fingers. "Lead the way."

We continued up the slope beside the cabin for a few

hundred more yards until we came to an old fire road. "Looks like they keep this clear just in case," Santiago said.

That was pretty typical up here near the park. Lots of roads were kept brush-free just in case fire broke out and emergency workers needed more points of access. I glanced back down the hill to where I could just see the moss-covered metal roof of the cabin. "We might have just walked up the wagon access to the house," I said.

Santi glanced back. "Could be," he said. "You got a source for old maps?" He winked at me since he already knew the answer to my question.

"I might be able to find something." I took out my phone to check for a signal. I had just enough to pull up the cache of images I kept of old maps. I looked closely at the one from the early twentieth century and zoomed in using GPS to pinpoint our location. "Sure enough," I said and held the phone up for Santiago to see.

"So this road goes right up to the ridge and down the other side to Elkton and then onto Harrisonburg." He studied the image and then spun my hand back to me. "Right?"

"Yeah," I said as I zoomed in even further. "Looks like it parallels Route 33, but even on this map, the road isn't very big. I'd say it was just a wagon road, probably for logging."

People up here had found ways to make money off the land whenever possible, and I knew a lot of the folks in this part of the mountains had made their money harvesting tree bark and selling it down in the valley.

"Think it goes through?" he asked me as he looked up the logging road toward the ridgeline.

I slid my fingers over the image. "Sure seems like it did at one time. One sec," I said as I opened up the map app on my phone. "It's hard to tell, but it seems like it might be passable now."

We walked a bit further up the road toward the west, and

after a few yards Santi stopped and bent down. "These don't look that old," he said pointing to tire tracks. He followed them back the way they came and then said, "Yep, they turned around right here." He gestured almost directly to the trail we'd just come up. "Looks like we have our entry point."

"Does this mean we're going four-wheeling?" I asked with a grimace.

His face broke into a wild smile. "You know it." He glanced at me. "And don't even think about declining the opportunity. I need your maps."

"I can just give you my phone, you know?" I said nervously.

"Nope. I need your navigation skills." We headed back toward the cabin. "It's only one p.m. The guys from search and rescue will have a Nebula up here in half an hour."

"A Nebula?" I asked, already bracing for the answer.

"The team's new UTV. It's so fast." His grin was as wide as his whole face.

I sighed.

"It'll be fun," he said, but his glee made me think his definition of fun and mine were not the same at all.

FORTY-FIVE MINUTES later I was in a police-issue jacket, gloves, and hat, going what I considered to be far too fast on the dirt road through the woods. Santiago was driving our UTV, and Savannah and Saul were following behind in another. Saul had sent his crew home but insisted on coming along. "I'm not missing a ride through the woods, and you know that," he'd said.

I'd offered to give him my seat in Santi's vehicle, but Santi had said I would prefer riding with him. "Savannah is a demon in one of these," he said.

He wasn't wrong. At one point, the road got just wide enough for Savannah to pass us, and she did...at speed. I yelped when she and Saul flew by, three hands in the air and delight on their faces. They were having so much fun that I decided to let myself enjoy it, too. "You better catch her," I shouted to Santiago.

He looked over at me briefly and then said, "You sure?"

I nodded before I could change my mind, and Santiago pressed the pedal down, launching us ahead. We rode along for a good quarter mile before Savannah stopped in front of us and pointed to the right. Just off the path was a camo-print tent with a carefully laid firepit out front. It looked like it had been there a good while, given the fading on the canvas, but it didn't look abandoned.

We turned off the machines and walked toward the tent, Saul and I letting the officers lead the way. Someone had definitely been living here; even I could tell that as we walked up. There was a trail to what looked like a makeshift outhouse behind the tent, and next to it, someone had rigged up a canvas tarp. Beneath the tarp was a metal shelf full of canned goods. This was someone's home.

As Savannah and Santi carefully made their way around the tent to the entrance, Saul and I retreated back up the small trail toward the UTVs. Unfortunately, we were well-seasoned in knowing police procedure, and that procedure didn't include us marching in on a potential suspect and complicating the situation.

It only took a couple of minutes, and then Savannah gave us the all-clear. "They've moved on. Looks like no one's been here in a few days."

Saul and I traipsed back down to the tent and watched as our friends gathered evidence – a hairbrush, a book that looked like a journal, and a few scraps of paper from the trash. I wanted to reach over and grab all the paper to look through it. But I restrained myself and trusted that if I could help with anything, Santi would ask for my help.

Now, though, it was time to head farther up the road and leave the rest of this scene to be processed by the deputies from Orange County that Savannah had requested before we headed out. We had about an hour before I had to pick up my son, and the most crucial thing, according to Santi, was that we figure out where this road came out.

Back in the UTVs, we made our way up the hill, all of us scanning the sides of the roadway for more residential spaces. We didn't see anything, but only about a half-mile past the tent, we came to a metal gate. Beyond it, a two-lane road ran perpendicular to ours. The Blue Ridge Parkway, as I had expected.

The Parkway is a closed road with very limited entrances that are monitored by park rangers. But if you'd lived around here long, you knew that there were also all these fire roads or simply old roads that hadn't grown in yet that intersected with the roadway. Many of them had been turned into hiking trails, and almost all of them were closed to vehicles by gates just like this one. But from what Santiago told me, a lot of UTVs and dirt bikes just went around those gates if they weren't closely monitored. He spent a fair amount of time, especially in the summer, working with the rangers to track down people joyriding from the roads onto the Parkway without paying the entrance fee or attending to the traffic laws up there.

We turned off the vehicles and stepped up onto the road. Savannah jogged one direction and Santi went the other, and within five minutes, they were both back to tell us we were between mile posts 7 and 8, a bit south of the entrance at Skyline Drive. "Guess this is how they got in with the body?" I said, feeling a little obvious.

"Yeah, it looks like this is kind of a well-used trail for hikers and some vehicles, too," Savannah said as she knelt near the ground. "Going to be hard to tell what is what."

"But there were no tire marks near the tent, so I expect that person was walking in and out." Santiago stared back down the mountain. "The tent and the body may not be related at all."

Saul huffed and then said, "Oh, sorry." But when Santiago continued to stare at him, he said, "You can't really believe that, right? I mean, a dead body in an abandoned cabin on the same road as someone's summer home..."

Santiago nodded. "You're right, Saul. But I can't make any assumptions, so I need to explore the avenues separately and let a connection arise."

"I got it. But you know there's a connection." Saul laughed.

Santiago rolled his eyes. "The other thing we need to consider is that someone might have gotten the body in via the road you made, Saul. When did you clear that?"

"Yesterday," Saul said, "but I dropped two huge logs across it overnight. Someone would have needed to use big equipment to move them, and I saw no signs of that."

Savannah looked around. "So we have our way in, but why here? I mean there are other places that are more accessible but just as abandoned, maybe more so if this camper isn't related to the crime."

Something was pinging in the back of my mind, but my practice with this sort of investigation told me that if I chased the noise, I'd lose the thread. I just made a mental note to hold onto Savannah's question as the investigation continued. It would all come together sometime.

The ride down was far less nerve-racking in terms of the investigation, but Savannah and Santiago made sure to up the adrenaline ante by flying down the road at top speed. All I could do was hang on for dear life and make Santiago promise not to take Sawyer for a ride like that until he was at least my age.

. . .

When I picked Sawyer up from school, he was all words, a whole frenzied bundle of words. He wanted to tell me about how they "always" do this at school and they "always" do that, and I let myself enjoy his monologue because it was, for the first time, a chance for him to tell me something about his life that I didn't already know. It made me a bit sad but mostly just happy. He had loved his day, and he was so excited to go back in "one sleep."

The whole ride home he kept slipping between the kind of reverie he went into when he was really tired and the need to tell me about something else that happened, from his new best friend Winston to the fact that he ate his entire roast beef sandwich at lunch but had traded his raisins for goldfish. He had all these stories, and I could tell he was weighing them like I did – what did he keep for himself and what did he share. It was a good lesson for him to consider.

Between his talking jags, I was pondering much the same thing. On the ride back from the cabin, Santiago and I had talked on the phone so that he could get a bit more information about the cabin, the O'Malley family, and Frank especially. "What's your sense, Pais? Is he involved?"

I had taken a deep breath as I turned onto the small road in the industrial park where Sawyer's school was located. "I don't think so, Santi. I really don't, but I've learned from you not to rule anyone out." I had paused before asking my question because I knew it might put my boyfriend in a difficult position. "You think I could tell him, though? I mean you could, should be there and everything, but this is going to be a big shock for him, I think. And it might be easier for him to take coming from me instead of the police."

The pause on the other end of the line had been long, but then he'd said, "Someday, I'm just going to need to permanently deputize you, you know?"

I had smiled and taken that as a yes. But now, as I thought

back over our conversation and our plan to go see Frank first thing tomorrow, I wasn't sure what I should share with the owner and what I shouldn't. Obviously, he had to know we'd found a body, but I didn't know if it would be wise or dangerous to tell him about the tent. I knew Santiago would coach me, but I also knew he'd give me a lot of leeway. I didn't want to damage the investigation with my big mouth.

Sawyer was so tired when we got home that he ate his dinner – a new favorite, chili – without complaint, played outside with Beauregard for a bit, and then went to bed a half hour early. My boy was tuckered.

Given that I was a bit frazzled by the day, I decided to use the evening to do a little more work on the O'Malley family. Sometimes disappearing into genealogical records was just the sort of intensely focused effort I needed to calm my mind and help me see new paths forward.

I started with Frank and put in the information he had given me about himself, his parents' names, and the names of his siblings, Shawn and Freya. Then, I began moving backward, keeping in mind that Frank had told me it was his third-great-grandparents who had moved here from Ireland. When I got to that generation, I found immigration records from Ellis Island that recorded Ewan and Molly O'Malley.

With them identified, I began to trace them from New York, through Philadelphia, and then down to Virginia with a group of other Irish folks who had been recruited by the railroad.

That put them moving to Virginia in the mid-1850s. All those dates lined up with what I had estimated the age of the cabin to be – about 160-175 years old.

I jotted down all my notes, took a picture of the draft family tree, and sent it over to Frank, hoping it would give him a little lift after the bad news of the day. At least when we showed up at his house tomorrow, we would talk about more than a murder victim.

With my work done, my nerves a little less frenzied but my mind still turning over the events of the day, I turned to my regular soothing task – cross-stitch. Lately, I'd been following folks on Instagram who cross-stitched, and I was amazed at the kind of output they had. One woman had cross-stitched an entire tapestry where every millimeter was a stitch. That would have taken me my entire lifetime, and even then I would have been passing the unfinished project on to Sawyer in my will. But this woman, she'd finished this in two years. In my mind, I imagined she was retired to a northern clime where she had great indoor lighting, below-zero temperatures, and twenty-four hours of darkness for nine months of the year. Probably such a place doesn't exist, but it made me feel better about my slow stitching speed to think it did.

My latest project was one just for me, a special tree of life pattern that was colorful but also simple. So many of the trees of life only contained the part of the tree above the soil line. This one, though, showed how strong and vibrant the roots were, too, and lately, I'd been really thinking about how much of health and wholeness in life come from things we don't always see.

Tonight, I was moving into the second row of the root system. I hadn't long been stitching with the parking method, but now that I had picked up this practice, I found it to be really fulfilling, to watch the pattern emerge like one of those draw-by-the-box games from when I was a child. This process took me longer, maybe, but it also saved me the frustration of always losing my place and having to pull out large numbers of stitches.

I threaded my needle with a bright-pink shade and began to stitch. Something was needling – pun fully intended – at me about the way that man's body had been lying. I knew what all the shows said about how the fact that a body being covered showed remorse by the killer, and while Santiago had told me that wasn't always the case, there was something about how this guy was set into this dry space – this place that had obviously been a home – that really struck me. Whoever had brought that man there had wanted him safe.

That idea haunted me long after I closed my eyes next to Sawyer that night.

3

I slept fitfully, but fortunately, Sawyer's first day of school had made him so tired that even my tossing and turning didn't affect him. When we both finally crawled out of bed with about twenty minutes to spare before we had to leave for school, he looked at me and said, "Mama, I slept like I was a log."

I laughed. "You did sleep like you were a log, Love Bug. You were tired." I hugged him close and took a deep breath of the scent of him. "How are you feeling about school today?"

He put a finger to his chubby cheek, like he always did when he wanted to seem pensive but already knew what he wanted to say, "Well, Mama, you know I'll miss you...but I love school, especially the pouring part."

"Pouring? Like pouring water?" I asked.

"It's an important skill, Heather says." His face was so serious as he mimicked what his teacher had told him, and I had to agree with Heather myself. Pouring was an important skill. The sticky spots on my floor were a testament to the fact that Saw needed a bit more in that skill area.

This time when I dropped him off, Saw didn't even want me to walk him to the door, so I waved from beside the car, took a deep breath to pull my tears back in, and called Santi. "You ready?" I asked when he picked up.

"As I'll ever be. You almost here?" He sounded tired, and I imagined he was. It had probably taken him most of the night to deal with the paperwork and reports on the body and the campsite.

"Be there in five. You want me to drive?" I was pretty sure his answer was going to be no because of the nature of our visit to Frank, but I wanted to offer.

"The cruiser is better for today. Just park out back." He disconnected, and a couple of minutes later I pulled in behind the police station, locked my car, and climbed into the passenger seat of his car.

"Hi, Beautiful," he said and kissed me on the cheek. "You ready?"

"As I'll ever be," I echoed and fastened my seatbelt. We rode for a few minutes in silence, and then I tried to lighten the mood. "So are you good cop, or bad cop?"

He cut me a glance from the corner of his eye and said, "This question implies that there are two cops in this car, and there is only one." He grinned, but the tightness in his jaw told me he was mostly serious. "I'll handle the questions, Pais, okay?"

I sighed. "You're right. Okay. How can I help?" When his hand slid over mine, I let out a long breath.

"Both Frank and I will appreciate you being there. And we need your historical perspective to get this thing together. Be you, Pais. Just be you." He lifted my fingers to his mouth and kissed them lightly.

I put my head back against the seat and closed my eyes. It felt like it had been a long time since anyone just wanted me for me, not for how I could hold them up or get them chocolate milk or say what they wanted me to say. I knew Santi meant what he said, in this context and more broadly, too, but I had to make a very concerted effort to believe him.

Still, when we got to Frank's beautiful farm on the edge of town, I felt calm and ready for whatever came, which was really saying something since we were here to talk about a murder.

Frank invited us into his cozy dining room, and we sat at the table while he poured us cups of coffee from his fancy pour-over carafe. "Nancy at school today?" Santi asked as he accepted the cream-colored mug that Frank handed him.

"Yep," Frank said with a smile. "How she can enjoy teaching middle school science I will never know." He handed me my own blue ceramic mug and sat down next to me. "It's all hormones and body odor at that age."

I laughed. "Maybe the smell of sulfur is an improvement, then?" Nancy O'Malley taught eighth grade chemistry at our county middle school. She'd been Teacher of the Year several times, and she had, without a doubt, more patience and good humor than anyone I'd ever met.

"Anything might be an improvement over hangdog yearning and the gap between never showering and always showering that seems to hit every pubescent boy at some point?" Santi snickered. "My mother has always marveled at how quickly I passed from hiding when it was time to shower to having to be forced out by a quick shutoff of the hot water valve."

This image brought Santi's mother to my mind. She was a stout, strong woman who had no trouble managing both her household and her business as the county's best seamstress, and I admired all that about her. But more, I was enamored with her softness, the way her strength didn't make her hard but instead seemed to allow her to ease in. Come to think of it,

Frank's wife had that quality, too. Strong but tender. I was going to have to ponder that some more.

Now, though, we had business to take care of, and when I looked over at Santi, he put his mug down and said, "Frank, we need to know if you had any idea that man's body was in your cabin."

Frank shook his head. "I didn't. You have my word. I just can't figure out why someone put him there." He looked up at us. "That's what you said, right? Someone put his body there?"

Santi nodded. "Looks like it. We think they might have come down from the Parkway on that logging road."

A band of red began to rise above Frank's collar, and I felt Santi tense beside me. "Something we need to know there, Frank?"

Frank let out a long sigh. "Everybody used to take that road to get in and out once we were up there. We'd take our UTVs behind our trucks and then go in and out that way. It's just so much faster."

Santiago sighed. "It's not uncommon, Frank, and really, the Park Service is responsible for closing off access. My guess is that they don't care that much."

"Yeah, and given that they displaced us in the first place..." I could hear the tinge of anger behind Frank's words, and I really couldn't blame him. The government had taken his family's land, their heritage in a sense.

"Frank," I asked, "did you get a chance to look at the family tree I sent over?" When he nodded, I said, "Everything seem accurate?"

"As far as I know. The names are familiar, and the timeline looks good. Daddy never talked much about the older generations. I never knew if that was because he didn't know anything or if the story of losing the cabin and farm just overwhelmed everything else." Frank rubbed his forehead. "But yeah, what you sent looks right."

I met his gaze. "I didn't want to pry too much into the people alive now. I respect people's privacy, but I did wonder who else might have a claim – if only in their hearts – to the cabin. Any cousins or anything?"

Santiago's leg slid over against mine, a small affirmation that being me was just what he needed now.

As he raised his arms over his head and cradled them at the base of his skull, Frank looked up at the ceiling. "We are Irish Catholic, you know?" he said with a small smile. "There are O'Malleys everywhere. I probably have six thousand cousins that I've never met but who look just like me." Frank sat forward. "Only three around here though that would, I'd guess, even know about the family cabin."

Santi took his small notebook from his breast pocket. "I'll need their names."

Frank listed three of the most Irish names I'd ever heard – well, besides Frank O'Malley – and I grinned as I got a silly image of Frank and his cousins Irish dancing at the county fair. Given that Frank was wearing mud-caked workboots instead of lightweight dancing shoes, I couldn't really see him leaning into that part of his cultural heritage, but I was enjoying the thought.

Apparently, I was enjoying it too much because Santi said, "What are you smirking about?"

I blushed and then confessed my strange imagining. "Sorry. I've been watching too much of these Irish brothers dancing on TikTok."

"The Gardiner Brothers," Frank said without hesitation. "They're amazing. Almost make me want to put tips on my boots." He laughed out loud then, and something of the tension in the room dissipated. "But my cousin Patrick" – he tapped a finger on Santi's notebook next to his cousin's name – "he does that kind of thing. All into the Irish heritage."

Santi nodded. "Well, that's good to know. Might be an icebreaker when I talk to him."

"If you can put on a wee Irish accent that'll help, too, lad," Frank said in his own mock brogue. "He's all in for Irish stuff."

"I feel like I might slip and start sounding like my mother, and Mexican English and Irish English probably don't sound alike." Santi laughed. "But thanks for the tip."

I glanced over at Santiago, and then said, "Frank, did you know someone was camping up above the cabin? Looks like they've been there a while."

This time a flush traveled all the way up to the roots of Frank's dark hair, and I knew we were on to something.

"I wondered if you'd find her. She okay?" Frank said.

"Find who?" Santiago asked. "The campsite was abandoned."

A look of alarm flashed over Frank's face. "Oh no," he said. "That's not good." He started to stand up and head toward the rotary phone on the wall. "Sorry, I have to make a call."

Santiago started to rise, to stop him I expected, but then he sat back down and took a sip of his coffee.

"Harriet, it's Frank O'Malley. Could you ask Nancy to call me as soon as possible?" He paused a moment. "Thanks."

Frank sat back down. "I really need Nancy to explain the situation to you since it's about one of her former students." He pulled his hands through his hair. "This isn't good."

I am not, by nature, a patient person, and I was about to ask Frank to tell us what he did know when the phone on the wall rang. Frank leaped up and answered. "Nancy, Santiago Shifflett and Paisley Sutton are here. They saw Katherine's campsite. She's not there."

He took a deep breath. "Okay. We'll be here." He hung up the phone and turned to us. "Nancy will be home in ten minutes. She's going to need to file a missing persons report."

I was rifling through the approximately twenty million

questions in my head, but given the way that both Santiago and Frank had gone into that type of male silence that feels like a locked bank safe, I figured I was going to have to wait.

So I did what all my Southern upbringing had taught me to do. I made myself at home, started a fresh pot of coffee, and opened cabinets until I found a tub of biscotti to put out with them. From the look on Frank's face and Nancy's willingness to leave school at a moment's notice, I figured we were going to need both caffeine and sustenance for the rest of the day.

LESS THAN TEN MINUTES LATER – Nancy must have been hauling in her little purple Prius – we were all seated at the table with fresh mugs of coffee and a biscotti each. As one who never could turn down anything with even a smidge of sugar, I was already crunching away when Nancy began to tell us about the woman from the campsite.

"Her name is Katherine Forester. She graduated last year from Octonia High. I've known her since she was thirteen years old. Great kid...horrible home life." Nancy took a deep breath. "She held out until she was eighteen just because she didn't want to end up in the system and couldn't afford the legal fees to emancipate, but she's been basically living with friends since she was twelve."

I shuddered. "It was that bad at home?"

"Worse than you can imagine. Her dad and stepmom had major issues, but not the kind people really saw. No addictions or anything that could be treated. Just absolute ugliness in their souls." Nancy cracked her knuckles as she took another deep breath. "Mind you, I don't like to talk ugly about anyone, but these people, well, they are monsters."

It was only at that moment that I realized Santiago hadn't moved a muscle since Nancy started talking. I looked over at him, and all the color had drained from his face. "Santi?" I said as I put a hand on his arm.

"We've been trying to help Katherine for almost a decade," Santiago said. "But nothing stuck to her parents. Teachers you included, Nancy – filed reports, and neighbors sent us pictures of what looked like Katherine being smacked around." Santiago let out a long sigh. "Millicent and Robert Forester are just as slick as spring mud. Every time we'd bring them in, they'd spin some story about what the neighbors 'must have thought' was going on. They'd talk about how they appreciated all the concern for their daughter but that she just had an 'overactive imagination.'"

Nancy groaned and said, "When I found a row of inch-long burns along Katherine's arms one day, they told me she'd been climbing the chain-link fence at the park and that it was just hot enough from the sun to burn her that way."

I cringed. Sawyer climbed every metal structure in the world, and even when the slide, or the fence, or whatever it was, burned to the touch, it never left him with visible burn marks. Never. This story was getting worse and worse. "What did Katherine say happened?"

"She didn't. Most of the time she simply parroted whatever story her parents had given her to say. She was scared." Nancy wrung her fingers together. "Once, though, when I saw a long bruise across her back when she bent over to tie her shoe and I asked her about it, she said her stepmom hadn't liked the way she was watering the garden and smacked her with the hose."

I gasped and wiped the tears that welled in my eyes away. This wasn't the time for me to get emotional. "That is so horrible." My words felt so weak in the light of what had happened to this child. "So when she could get away..."

"She did. She didn't have much money, but she was the most resourceful person I knew." Nancy looked at Frank. "I took her class up to the cabin once to look at native plants, and

Katherine had loved it up there. She went up the mountain anytime she could, with us sometimes but often by herself."

"So when she was legally an adult, she decided to live in the woods?" Santiago asked.

Frank nodded. "She asked permission from us, and we were glad to give it. We kept an eye on her, took her food from time to time, but she had a job down here in town at the grocery store and never needed much."

"It was the happiest I'd ever seen her," Nancy said. "She thrived up there."

"When was the last time you saw her?" Santiago asked.

Nancy said, without hesitation, "Last Tuesday. That's when you took up those pots you found at the SPCA thrift, right?"

Frank nodded. "Yeah, Katherine had mentioned a few weeks ago that she had cooked through the bottom of her saucepan, so I grabbed a couple of cheap ones to take to her. Tuesday the weather was so nice that I made the trek up."

"And she was there?" I asked as I found myself thoroughly caught up in this young woman's story.

"Yep. On her day off from the store and busy dyeing yarn made from some of the fleece I'd given her. She was quite the spinner, and she hoped to sell some of her yarn to that store in town." Frank gazed across the room. "She had used purple asters to produce the dye, and it was lovely. I can say that even though I'm not a man that into yellow." Frank gave us a half-smile.

I swallowed hard and hoped this young woman would get a chance to have Mika stock her yarn. I knew my best friend would love to help someone out, but she also loved a good hand-dyed yarn and could sell it at a premium during the summer season. It was then that something struck me. "I didn't see any yarn in her tent, did you?"

Santiago shook his head. "No. I wasn't looking for that, but I expect I would have noticed if skeins were hanging up around a tent. And I know you would have noticed."

I nodded vehemently. "Definitely." I looked over at Nancy. "Do you think she might have gathered enough of a lot to be bringing it down to sell?"

Nancy shrugged. "Maybe. She spun with a drop spindle, so she wasn't fast. But she didn't have much else to do up there, so maybe."

I met Santiago's eyes, and when he nodded, I said, "My best friend Mika runs the yarn shop in town. We'll go check with her, see if she saw Katherine."

When I looked over at Nancy, I saw tears in her eyes. "Thank you. And what do I do to formally file a report?" She looked over at Santiago.

"Nothing further, except if you have a recent picture, I could use that. I'll put out the word. She hasn't been up there in a few days at least," he said gently, "so it's time for us to begin searching."

We all stood up then, and I hugged Nancy tight. "I'll tell you as much as I can as we go, okay?"

Santiago smiled at me and then at them. "We both will." He shook Frank's hand. "If you think of anything else that's relevant about the cabin, you'll let me know?"

Frank nodded. "Of course, and do you want me to give my cousins a heads-up that you'll be calling or just leave that be?"

"Not trying to sneak up on anyone, but let's leave it be. Sometimes people can be more honest when they don't have time to overthink things," Santiago said with a small smile. "Thanks for asking that."

"Understood," Frank said as he held the back door open for us. "We'll let you know what we find, too."

Santi paused and looked at the couple. "Just be careful, okay? Someone has been killed. Be smart."

Nancy nodded. "Always am, Sheriff." She smiled and then watched us walk around the house to Santiago's car.

Once we were on the road, I said, "Mika or the grocery store first?"

"Both. You okay talking to Mika on your own?" He grinned at me. "She can be a hard nut to crack."

"I think I can handle her," I said. And I hoped I was right.

4

Mika and I had been best friends for decades now, and if anyone knew how I operated in the world, it was her, and vice versa. But sometimes, Mika got a little cagey when it came to her business, not because she had something to hide but because she wasn't always confident that her business choices were sound. Given that the yarn store was blowing up, both in person and online, and that she'd been able to hire two employees to help manage things, I think it was safe to say she was just fine in the business department. But I wasn't the one who needed to be convinced of that.

So while I felt fairly certain that Mika would be really forthright about Katherine if the young woman had been in, especially since she was now missing, there was always the slim chance that my friend would clam up if she'd bought the woman's yarn but thought maybe she'd overpaid or something. The only way I'd know was to ask.

When Santiago dropped me off on the sidewalk outside her door, I practically ran in. If there was one thing I knew about my best friend was that she had a huge heart that was easily carried along by someone else's emotions. It wasn't her best quality, we both knew, but it was exciting to have good news to share with her because she was always even more excited than I was.

Today, though, the tide of emotion wasn't going to be positive, and while I was eager to tell her what we'd found, I also didn't relish reliving the discovery of either the man's body or the news about Katherine's parents and their abuse. Still, Mika was a good listener, so maybe it would help.

As soon as I swung open the door, both Mika and her assistant Mrs. Stephenson looked up with genuine smiles on their faces, smiles that grew broader when they saw it was me. Mrs. Stephenson was a retired accountant, and when Mika had hired her to help clerk the shop, she'd gotten a bookkeeper, marketing assistant, and clerk in one. The two women were bent over one of the tables near the front of the store looking at what appeared to be a magazine, and when they closed the magazine quickly as I approached, I guessed they'd been discussing a project for my birthday next month. Either that or planning a coup, but something yarn-related was more likely. Maybe.

"Didn't know we'd see you today, Paisley!" Mrs. Stephenson said as I walked over, dropped my bag, and immediately grabbed a soda from the small cooler Mika kept in the Cozy Nook. "How's Sawyer liking school?"

"Liking it?" I said after a long pull on the Pepsi can. "He loves it. I think he'd move in with his teacher Heather if he could. They did pouring yesterday."

"A crucial skill," Mrs. Stephenson said as she deftly slid the magazine into a roll and headed toward the register. "I'll let you two catch up."

How that woman could always read a room so well I'll never understand, but I was especially grateful for her astuteness at that point. Mika grabbed her own soda – a Diet Dr. Pepper – and slid into the wingback chair beside me. She popped the tab on her can, took a sip, and said, "Okay, so give me all the news."

I'd updated Mika briefly by text the day before because, well, that's just what we did. Texts were our adult equivalent of passing notes in class – it's how we stayed close even if we weren't spending a lot of time together.

I told her about Frank's cousins and about Patrick, the lover of all things Irish. Then, I filled her in on Katherine Forester and her family story. Mika gasped and teared up, as I expected she would. "We should tell Mrs. Stephenson. She might know something."

I nodded but put my hand on her arm when she started to stand. "First, though, I need to ask you something. I don't think you know, but you have a tie to Katherine Forester."

Mika tilted her head. "I do?"

"She spun yarn and hand-dyed it. Her last batch was a light yellow dyed with aster petals."

A gasp hissed between Mika's lips. "Her yarn is gorgeous." She jumped up and ran to the back room and then returned with a small box of exquisite wool yarn that she placed in my lap. "Something told me I needed to help her, so I bought all she had, even though it's not really enough for me to sell yet." A little color crept into Mika's face. "I know that's not the best business investment–"

I put up a hand. "Stop it. You do not ever need to explain your kind heart to me. She did need the money, and you helped her a great deal. And she probably needs your help now. When was she here?"

Mika let her head drop back against the chair. "It was in the past week, I think." She popped up again. "Hold on." She jogged over to the counter where Mrs. Stephenson stood and pulled out a ledger book. I had made fun of Mika for keeping her purchase records in a book like that at first, but when Mrs. Stephenson had said that it helped most people to see their spending in black and white, I had stopped. And I'd also bought myself a ledger to use. Mrs. Stephenson knew her stuff.

Both women came back over to where I was, Mika with ledger in hand, and sat down. Mika scanned a short list of entries and then said, "It was Friday afternoon of last week." She looked up at me. "She came in just after lunch."

I nodded and texted the information to Santiago. The timeline for when Katherine had disappeared had just been cut in half, and I knew that was a good thing in all the ways.

"Do you remember anything else about her? Anything that stood out?"

Mrs. Stephenson looked from me to Mika and back. "She looked thin, too thin, but otherwise no, nothing." The older woman studied me for a minute. "Did you say she was living in a tent?"

I nodded. "For more than a year now, it sounds like."

"She was clean. I remember asking her what shampoo she used because her long brown hair smelled lovely." Mrs. Stephenson laughed. "She told me it was rain water and cloves with a little castile soap. Homemade."

"She makes her own shampoo?" I said. "Wow. She is hardcore."

"Exactly what I thought," Mika added, "when she told me she drop-spun her yarn and hand-dyed it with foraged dyes. All that work, and she wanted to charge me five dollars a skein. I insisted that she needed to take double, and even then I'd still make a fifty percent markup." Mika sighed. "I felt kind of bad that I hadn't paid her more, after she left, but I made a note right here to offer her twelve-fifty a skein next time."

I smiled. "I'm sure she was grateful for the income. I don't know what she makes at the grocery store, but most of us can use a little extra cash."

Mrs. Stephenson's brow furrowed. "She works at the grocery store. I haven't ever seen her there. Have either of you?"

Now that she mentioned it, I hadn't, and it seemed Mika hadn't either. I did most of my shopping at the larger grocery stores closer to Charlottesville, but I was in our local IGA at least once a week for little things like chocolate milk or a loaf of bread. But I hadn't seen her.

"Never," Mika said. "When she came in here, it was the first time I'd seen her."

I nodded. When the O'Malleys had handed Santi the photo of them with Katherine that was taken back in the winter on a snowy day I hadn't even had an inkling that the young woman looked familiar. In a place as small as Octonia, that was saying something. "That's odd, right? That we didn't recognize her."

The three of us sat quietly with the strangeness of that fact for a few moments. Then Mrs. Stephenson said, "I'm calling the O'Malleys. Time to get organized, ladies."

I smiled. Mrs. Stephenson was a force, and between her and Nancy O'Malley, there was no way Katherine Forester was going to stay missing. I could feel it.

While Mrs. Stephenson made her call and Mika took care of a pair of middle-aged women who wanted yarn for a stress-relief project, I jumped online to see what I could find about Katherine Forester and her family. Surprisingly, there wasn't much to find. Not even social media profiles for her parents or anything. One article in the local paper mentioned her parents as part of a fundraiser at their church, but that was it. Nothing else out there.

I was just going to start digging a little deeper into the family history with some genealogical sites when Santiago came back in and dropped heavily into the chair beside me. "This woman is like a ghost," he said as he stared up at the ceiling.

"We were just saying the same thing," I said. "None of us has ever seen her at the grocery store."

"Nope, you wouldn't have," he said as he dropped his eyes

to mine. "She was the warehouse manager. She did receiving, but she refused to work the floor."

I looked at him and tried to imagine myself as a young woman working in a small grocery store. At least on the floor, I'd have been able to talk to people from time to time, and as introverted as I was, human contact was important to me. But apparently, avoiding it was more important to Katherine. Then, with a thud, a realization hit me. "She didn't want to risk seeing her parents."

Santi nodded. "That's what I'm thinking, too. Her manager said she was phobic about even having to come into the front of the store. She came in and left through the back door, even, and when she needed to buy things for herself, the manager shopped, and then she paid him for her purchases."

"Sounds like an accommodating manager," I said.

"He said she was the best worker he'd ever had, and it sounded like he meant it." Santiago sighed. "I wish we'd been able to help her when she was a kid."

I leaned over and put my hand on his knee. "I know you did everything you could. But maybe we can help her now." I pointed toward where Mrs. Stephenson was making notes on a sheet of paper by the register. "Mrs. Stephenson is talking to the O'Malleys. They're going to organize a search."

"Just talked to Frank. We're going back up to the woods this afternoon with volunteers. Want to come?" Santiago stood up. "We could pick up Sawyer on the way."

I finished my soda and then dropped the can in the recycling bin. "A chance to help and be in the woods might just be enough to convince Sawyer to leave school. I'll see if Dad and Lucille are free, too."

"Cool. Give me fifteen and then meet me at the station," he said as he squeezed my shoulders and headed for the door.

I nodded and then texted Sawyer's preschool to let them

know I'd be by a couple of hours early. His teacher Heather replied immediately, *See you soon.*

I told Mika about the search, and as I finished, Mrs. Stephenson hung up. "I'll staff the shop if you want to go, Mika. I can coordinate the volunteers from here...if you don't mind."

"Don't mind at all," Mika said as she put her phone in her back pocket. "Use anything from the store you need – paper, copier, anything."

Mrs. Stephenson said a quick thanks and then jumped back on the phone, this time with what sounded a lot like a reporter, given the things Mrs. Stephenson was saying about Katherine: where and when she went missing, and remarks about the gathering search party.

By the time Mika and I walked down to the station, there was already a large gathering of officers, many off-duty from surrounding counties. They were all dressed in bright-orange vests and carried clipboards and flags. I'd never done a search before, but it looked like this one was well organized. I was glad because, suddenly, the weight of Katherine's disappearance felt very, very heavy.

Santiago had put his extra car seat in the back of his cruiser already, and to minimize the number of cars up the mountain, Savannah rode along with the four of us. Sawyer and his teacher were outside when we got to the small school, and as he ran toward me, Heather caught my attention. "I heard about Katherine. We'll join the search as soon as the rest of the parents get here. We're closing early."

I smiled. This was just the sort of thing Octonia was known for. We could drive each other up the wall with our political views and our squash casserole recipes, but when push came to shove, we showed up for each other. "Did you know her?"

Heather nodded. "From school. Nice girl. Kept to herself, but always kind to me." She waved as I headed back to the car. "See you up there."

If word had already reached the preschool, then I imagined we'd have a very large crowd at the Parkway. It was the easiest place to meet, Santiago said as we drove up into the mountains, because the Park Service had agreed to open the logging road for us. They were sending rangers to join the search, and they'd already begun hanging fliers and talking to campers and hikers around the park.

I couldn't help but wonder how the reclusive Katherine would feel about all these people looking for her and could only hope that our efforts would be rewarded. But something about this situation felt very ominous, dark, like a cloud lingering behind the mountain, ready to unload on all of us.

THE WEIGHT of our task was heavy on us all as we drove. At least, I presume it was heavy on everyone else, too, because no one, not even Sawyer, talked as we drove up the mountain. When we got close to the Parkway, I did explain to my son what was happening and that he and I would be looking together to see what we could find at Katherine's campsite. That had been the plan Santiago and I formulated to let Sawyer and me be involved but also keep him from potentially gruesome findings if this became more of a recovery mission.

"Okay, Mama," my son said. "We'll look for clues and help bring Heather's friend home."

I smiled at him and his tender heart and then sat back to try and let the mountains fill me up a bit as we drove the few miles to the gate by the logging road. But something about what Sawyer had just said unsettled me, and it took me almost the whole ride to realize it was that his teacher had told him the person missing was her friend.

I was a little bothered that his teacher had been talking to him about this at all – that felt a bit like overstepping – but it was more what she'd told Sawyer having led him to think of

Katherine as his teacher's friend that stuck with me. Given, Saw didn't have a real firm grasp of friendship yet but still, that he used that word but then his teacher had given the impression she and Katherine were mere school acquaintances gave me a bit of pause. I decided I'd tell Santiago about my ponderings later, though, because we needed all our wits about us now.

The crowd at the head of the road was enormous, a couple of hundred people milling about as the officers wrote down the names of the volunteers and began to order them into groups. Savannah jumped out to join the work immediately, but before Santi stepped out, he said, "You're all in my group. At the campsite. Just us."

His face was very serious, so despite the flow of questions running into each other at the back of my tongue, I kept my mouth shut and unbuckled Sawyer's seatbelt. I had thought it was just going to be Saw and me doing a thorough once-over at the campsite, but clearly, something was on Santiago's mind that warranted his presence and Mika's there, too.

Now wasn't the time to query about that either, so Saw, Mika, and I gathered in a clump at the edge of the crowd as Santiago found Savannah, took the megaphone from her hands, and began to give instructions to the volunteers. "This is a search mission for a missing woman. You have all been sent a photo of her so you can reference it if need be. She is a seasoned woodswoman, but even the most experienced person can make a mistake. Please keep your eyes and ears open and immediately report anything you find to the officer in charge of your team. Thank you for coming."

My boyfriend took his job very seriously in all situations, but the tenor of his voice and the stiffness of his gait told me he was carrying this one heavy. Murders were hard, but missing persons cases, especially when the missing person was a young woman with such a hard life, those were even harder. I didn't know how long we'd be out here today, but I told Santi I'd give him a massage the next time I had a chance.

Now, though, he gestured for us to follow him down the road, and given that he was moving at a quick pace, I gathered that he didn't want us to dawdle. We bustled after him with Mika giving Sawyer a piggyback ride, and by the time we caught up, we were almost out of sight of the other volunteers. "Slow down, Cowboy," I shouted. "Some of us don't have our running legs warmed up yet."

He paused and glanced back at me with a small smile. "Sorry. I didn't want anyone following us. We don't need more people in this area just yet."

I nodded and picked up my pace as I came alongside him. "Got it. Mika, you and Love Bug okay?"

Mika grinned. "I hadn't gotten my cardio in yet today, but I'm all set now. CrossFit has nothing on the Sawyer Sutton training program."

Over her shoulder, Saw grinned at me, but there was something subdued in his expression. "You okay, bud?" I asked.

"Are we going to find a dead body?" he asked.

Mika stopped and let him slide to the ground. Then he walked over to me slowly. "No, Love Bug. We're not." I bit my tongue as I started to explain the reasons we were going where we were and the hope that Katherine was still alive. Sometimes, things are better left unsaid, especially to preschoolers.

Santiago stepped forward and picked up my son. "Our job is super special. We need to look at where Ms. Forester lived and see if we can find any clues. Did you bring your magnifying glass?"

Sawyer's eyes got wide. "No. What am I going to do?"

"Fortunately, I thought ahead and figured you didn't have yours at school." He pulled a heavy magnifying glass out of the small bag that hung from his shoulder. "You can use this one."

With gravity, Saw took it from Santiago's hand and began to

peer around at the woods. "I'll keep an eye out," he said as he slipped to the ground with the glass to the forest floor.

I winked at Santiago. "Thanks," I said.

"No need to thank me. That child is working today." He smiled. "Sawyer, your job is to look for anything that doesn't belong, okay? So if it doesn't look like it's part of these woods naturally, you shout, and I'll come running."

"You bet," Sawyer said and put his eye back to the glass as he scoured the ground before him.

Within a couple of minutes, we arrived at the campsite, and Santiago immediately asked Sawyer to walk with me around the campsite to see what we could find. The two of us began our stroll of the perimeter with me scouring the woods and my son with his eyes locked on the ground beneath us. We had made it about two-thirds of the way in a circle around the site when Sawyer stopped in his tracks. He'd already found pieces of glass and a couple of shotgun shells, which I had carefully slipped into the plastic bag Santi had given me, but both of us knew those were probably unimportant.

Now, though, Sawyer shouted for Santiago, "I found something. Come see." He held his magnifying glass perfectly still, and when I looked over his shoulder, I saw what he saw: a hair tie. A blue one. Just like the ones I wore, and in it, there were several long brown hairs.

"Don't touch, Mama," Saw said, backing away. "It's evidence."

I suppressed a grin and gave him a solid nod. He was right, of course. This did look like evidence.

Santi jogged over, took one look at the clue, and gave Sawyer's hair a tousle. "Great work, Little Man," he said before bending down and carefully slipping the tie and the hairs into his own bag. Then, he was on the radio on his belt and telling Savannah to get the search teams to look south of the road.

Mika walked over and joined us. When Santiago held up the bag, she nodded. "Matches the ones in the tent," she said.

Santiago nodded. "You guys up for a grid search of our own?"

Sawyer's eyes lit up. "Yeah!" he said with a fist pump of enthusiasm. I was glad to see him happy, but I sure hoped this wasn't going to be my son's first time finding a body.

I caught Santi's eye, and he nodded slowly. He understood my fear, but he also knew time was of the essence. We couldn't wait until another team got here, not when we were already days behind in starting the search. "You lead the way," I said with a significant gaze at my boyfriend.

He nodded, and then he and Mika walked out about ten feet ahead of us, with a few feet between them. Sawyer and I split the middle and walked along, keeping our eyes peeled for other clues. I kind of wished I had my own magnifying glass, if I was honest.

It wasn't long before Santiago put his arm above his head and stopped. When we reached them, he was already using his tweezers to pick up a small gold bracelet. "Let me see that picture?" he said, gesturing toward the phone in my hand.

I opened the screen and held it up for him.

"Yep, this is hers, too." He looked in the direction we'd been heading. "Let's keep going."

This time, the four of us spread out a couple shoulders apart, with Sawyer taking his own line to track, and we moved slowly forward, our eyes on the ground. The third find was Mika's, a drawstring from a jacket or sweatpants or something. Santiago bagged this one, and when Sawyer spotted a piece of pink chewing gum right along the same line we'd been walking, it became very clear that Katherine Forester was Hanseling us with her own version of breadcrumbs.

As we continued to follow the young woman's trail, Santiago called Savannah and had the teams narrow their focus from the Parkway and logging road toward the direction we were. I wasn't great at directions, but I had the feeling we were going to intersect with the Parkway up ahead, so I asked Santiago why not send the teams ahead of us.

"Because," he said, "I want them to double-check our work, and if I'm right, there won't be much ahead of us to find."

I wasn't sure what he meant, but since he took off on our trail again without another word, I held my questions and took my position in our search.

Sure enough, in a couple of hundred yards, we came out on the Parkway by an overlook, where Mika found another hair tie, this one with a small piece of paper tucked inside. When Santiago picked it up, he carefully used the tweezers to open the paper and then read out loud, "Blue Durango."

"Well, I'll be," Santiago said with a smack to his leg. "She told us the make and model of her kidnapper's car. Smart girl," he said.

"Woman," Mika and I said in unison while Sawyer nodded.

"Right. Woman," Santi corrected. "All right, we can call off the search then. Or rather, we can retarget it."

"Time for a neighborhood BOLO for a blue Dodge Durango?" I asked.

"Fastest way to find a car in Octonia," Mika added.

"Darn tootin'," Santiago said. "Get texting, women."

5

By the time Savannah pulled up in the cruiser to pick us up, we'd already messaged everyone from Mrs. Stephenson to my dad and Lucille to Saul to let them know to spread the word about the fact that we were looking for a blue Dodge SUV.

Lucille and Dad had stayed back from the search to help Mrs. Stephenson organize a campaign to get fliers of Katherine up all over town, and now, they and the O'Malleys were going to add the information about the car to their efforts.

I had been surprised when Santiago had said he'd asked the O'Malleys not to come up the mountain and search, but when he told me they were going to go to see Katherine's parents I understood. They trusted Santiago to handle the search, but they didn't trust the Foresters as far as they could throw them.

As we drove back toward the Parkway entrance, we came across a mob of people blocking the road up by where the search had started. Two officers were in the middle of the crowd, and it was clear they were quickly losing control of the situation. "Stay here," Savannah said as she and Santiago jumped out of the car.

"No problem," Mika said. "I don't want to get squished by all those grumpy people, do you, Saw?"

"No way," he said emphatically as he studied the crowd through the car window. "They look really mad."

I agreed with my son. This crowd was livid. Fortunately, the megaphone and a few threats about having to use tear gas to disperse the group brought the rabble to a rest. I added a note to my ever-growing list of questions for Santiago to see if they actually carried tear gas.

As people began to move aside and return to their cars, Savannah climbed back into the driver's seat and moved the cruiser off the side of the road. "Sorry. It's going to be just a minute." She glanced into the rearview mirror to where Santiago stood talking to a middle-aged man and woman. He was wearing khakis and a polo shirt, and she was in a long broomstick skirt and a blouse. They looked like they'd just walked out of a 1990s commercial for car insurance. "Those are Katherine's parents."

Savannah got back out of the car, and I gawked through the back window at the nondescript couple who had caused their child so much pain. Some small part of me that had been churched into the belief that appearances would tell me something about people's character wanted to dismiss everything I'd learned about these two people because individuals looking this white-bread just could not be torturers. But then, the part of me that now was part of a church that believed in justice remembered that appearances can be deceiving, and just because someone would treat me well doesn't mean they would treat all people that way. My friend Mary and others at our church had taught me that about racism, and I figured it was probably true of child abusers, too.

The couple was speaking very calmly with Santiago, and

while I didn't really want anyone yelling in my boyfriend's face, I found it highly disconcerting that these people had just learned their daughter was missing and were so poised. If something had happened to Sawyer, I would have been a mess of tears and shouting and probably some chest pounding, too. These two looked like they were trying to negotiate a lower price for a car they didn't really care about buying.

I shot Mika a look, and she shook her head as if to say, *Those people are a real piece of work*, and I couldn't disagree with her. But I also didn't know how I'd explain that to Sawyer without sounding mean and cruel, so instead I said, "Way to go on finding clues, Little Man."

He beamed. "I'm a police officer," he said. "The youngest depatee."

"You are the youngest deputy, Love Bug." I kissed the top of his head and let him study my hand through the magnifying glass while we waited.

A few minutes later, both Savannah and Santiago got into the car, and as soon as their doors were closed, Santiago let loose. "Those people have some nerve," he said, then with a quick glance in the mirror he saw Sawyer staring at him. "Sorry, Little Man. I got a little angry, and I shouldn't have shouted."

"What did they do, Santi?" he asked.

Santiago looked at me in the mirror and I nodded. Sawyer knew Santi was upset, and it was better for him to understand why than to simply wonder. I trusted Santiago to give us the G-rated version of things for now.

"Those were the parents of the woman we were looking for, the one whose hair tie you found," Santi said.

"I bet they're worried," Sawyer said earnestly.

"You'd think, wouldn't you?" Santi snapped before taking a long deep breath. "They were a little worried. They wanted to know if they could get their daughter's things out of the woods."

I frowned into the mirror at Santi, and he rolled his eyes.

"Because they were worried they'd get ruined," Sawyer said.

"Maybe that's it, Saw-Guy. Maybe they didn't want her things to get ruined." In the mirror, though, I could tell Santiago didn't think that was the reason at all.

THE REST of the ride was fun because Sawyer had a lot of questions about what he had to do as the youngest "depatee" and because Mika and I thoroughly enjoyed watching Savannah and Santiago try to answer his questions in a way that a four-year-old would understand. When he asked if he could have his own pair of handcuffs, Santiago deftly explained that they'd have to get him a small pair so that it would fit any of the child criminals Sawyer might encounter. And when he followed up and said he'd need his own police car, too, Savannah said, "We'll have to requisition one for you, and that's a lot of paperwork. It might be a while."

Sawyer took all the information in stride and then said, "Mom, can you call Heather and tell her I have to work tomorrow so I can't come to school?"

I smiled. "My understanding is that your assignment is to keep an eye on things at your school, isn't that right, Officer Winslow?"

"Absolutely. We need you to report anything suspicious at your school, okay? You're our eyes and ears on the ground," Savannah said with a smile.

"You bet," Sawyer said before looking at me and saying, "Mama, I need a notebook like Santi's."

"You got it, Love Bug. We'll get you one when we get home." I loved his sincere enthusiasm for his new role, and I hoped Heather had a way to keep his police duties in check during story time. No one needed a nosy four-year-old taking notes on how many times everyone used the potty.

Santiago dropped Mika and Sawyer off at her shop so that I could go with him and Savannah to the station and get my car. Saw was convinced of this plan by the promise of a soda while he waited with Mika, and I was glad for the minute alone with the officers to get the scoop on what was up with the Foresters.

"So they actually wanted to go and claim their daughter's things? Why?"

"They said something about valuable family heirlooms," Savannah said with a roll of her eyes, "but I would guess they were hoping she had some money stashed in there."

"And she did," Santiago said with a smirk, "but I confiscated that as evidence." He took a deep breath. "I told them it was an active crime scene, and that we would let them know when and if they could claim any items. But that for them to have that claim, their daughter would have to relinquish her rights or be found dead."

I groaned. "Let me guess. They weren't too devastated by the idea that their child could have died."

"Didn't even blink," Savannah spat. "It was disgusting."

"Ugh," I said. "That's just cruel."

"And suspicious," Santiago said. "Let's give them the full look-see, shall we?" he said to Savannah.

"Absolutely." If I had any doubt that Savannah was passionate about her job, which I did not, it would have been dispelled by the way she strode into the station.

"Those people don't stand a chance," I said as I watched her walk away.

"No, they do not." Santiago rested his head against the seat. "It may be a late night."

"I hear that. Your choice. Come over whenever or go home. I'll understand either way." I really hoped he'd come home to me instead of to his house, but I was still just insecure enough in our relationship to not be able to say those actual words.

"How about I come home to you at your house?" he whispered as he leaned in to kiss me. "Would that be okay?"

Today had already been a lot, but those words unsealed the dam of my emotions. I started to cry, quietly but steadily. When I caught my breath and looked at him, I saw a tear on his cheek, too. "Yes, that would be absolutely okay," I said. "I already have your toothbrush in the cabinet."

He kissed me again, and then I got out of the car and went to pick up my son, feeling happy and sad and all the things that make us human.

6

I didn't even hear Santiago come in that night, but when I woke up about three a.m., I found him with his arms wrapped around Sawyer in the bed next to me. Even in that bleary moment, I was able to think two things clearly – this is what this is supposed to feel like, and we need to get a king-size bed. But then, I reached over, put my arm over both my boys, and fell asleep.

When I woke up a few hours later, I couldn't move my right arm, and Sawyer was poking me repeatedly in my face. But seeing Santi's sleepy grin as he reached to tickle my son was enough to make me put up with things far worse than pins and needles and face pokes.

It was a good thing, too, because as soon as we dropped Sawyer off at school and Santiago took me to my shop, I heard the update on the night and why Santiago hadn't come until after one a.m. Someone had vandalized Katherine's campsite.

"I had an officer on duty up on the Parkway, and we put a game camera by the cabin. But apparently someone was very stealthy and very determined because they made off with almost everything personal from the campsite." Santiago said as he prepped the coffee pot on the counter.

"The Foresters must really want something up there," I said as I straightened the shelves and half-heartedly ran a feather duster over everything.

Santiago handed me a mug of coffee and then sat down. "Well, we don't *know* it was them. All we could see was two people in black hooded sweatshirts on the game camera."

"Well, *you* don't know, but I know. Those people are monsters." Clearly, the stress of the week had pushed me past my desire to actually be generous to these people. "What did they take?"

"Everything that was personal. Clothing. Books. Even the trash." Santiago held his coffee to his face and let the steam float up.

"The trash?"

He nodded. "Yep, bagged up the little trash can she had and took the whole thing."

I sighed. "That seems a little excessive even for these people, don't you think?"

"Not if they want to hide something." He raised his eyebrows above his mug. "Their behavior definitely makes me more suspicious, though."

"You think?" I said as I sat down next to him. "So what's on the agenda for your day?"

"Well, Savannah has some information to share" – he glanced at me with a sideways grin – "which I will share with you if I can. Then, I'm going to spend some time with the O'Malleys and Mrs. Stephenson. They volunteered to spearhead the tip line about the Durango, so hopefully they'll have a lead."

"Wow, that's a lot. And you still have to investigate a murder?" I said it lightly, but I knew Santiago was taking all of these situations as anything but light.

"Yeah, but I expect we're going to find that a lot of these threads intersect." He drained his coffee mug and stood. "There is too much going on in that square mile of forest for things to not be connected."

I expected he was right, but he didn't need my affirmation in that regard. He knew he was good at his job. "Thanks for coming home last night," I said. "Maybe we can give some thought to making that a more permanent arrangement?" I winced internally as soon as I said it because the last thing Santiago needed to be worrying about right now was whether or not he wanted to move in with me and Sawyer.

"I was hoping you'd say that. I'll put a call into a realtor about selling my place." He leaned over, kissed me, and then walked out the door.

I was left staring at him and wondering if what I thought had happened had actually just happened.

The rest of the morning went by in a blur as I thought about waking up to Santi every morning, as I pondered how Sawyer's dad would feel about the arrangement, and as I took care of the couple of customers who came by and also packed up the things I'd sold online. By the time lunch rolled around, I was exhausted and exhilarated in equal measure.

So when Saul dropped by with meatball subs and sodas, I was grateful for the excuse to sit down and focus on one person instead of on all the things spinning inside my head. Unfortunately, Saul wasn't the type for small talk, and the silence was long and extended as we made our way through the subs.

Eventually, though, he said, "Sheriff tell you yet when we can go into the cabin?"

I shook my head. "He hasn't, and with all that's going on up there, it may be a bit yet. You have other work for the crew?"

When a slow smile broke across Saul's face, I braced myself. That look never meant good things. Well, it always meant good things, but it usually also meant those things were hard. "What?!"

"Well, you know that old farmhouse we took down a couple months back?"

I did know. It had been a beautiful two-over-two place with the original chimneys and lots of pumpkin pine floors through-out. Despite the fact that the building had been abandoned for ten years, everything – including the roof – had been in great shape. So we were able to take down the entire building, piece by piece, with the intention of selling it as a lot. "Yes? What about it?"

"Well, what if we rebuild it here on the lot and stage it with your wares?" His smile had gotten very wide, and he had a sort of joker-meets-cheshire-cat kind of vibe.

"What do you mean?" I asked, trying to figure out exactly what he was saying.

"You need more space, Pais, and if we move this shed to the back and use it for actual storage, we can put that house right here and give you all the room you need to display what you have." His smile was almost touching both his ears now.

"But that house is worth a lot of money, money we were going to split," I whispered.

"Well, it's not selling, and it may never sell. But if we put up that house, it'll be a big draw from the road, and we can put my office in one corner and tear down the metal building in the back to make room for more materials. It's a win-win." He was studying my face now, and his smile was a little smaller. "You don't like the idea?"

I shook my head, partially to disagree with him and partially to clear my head. "No, I do like the idea. I'm just trying to wrap my head around it." The house was just a little over 1600 square feet, which wasn't a lot of room, but it did have four separate spaces. One for Saul's office, one for my sales space, and two for displays. Plus, the antebellum structure would be a great marketing tool for what I did, since we'd taken it down and could reassemble it to show what was possible with a salvaged building. My smile started to match Saul's.

"Is that a yes, then?" he asked as he leaned toward me. "Say it's a yes, Paisley-girl."

I couldn't possibly say no to Saul's generous offer, and while I began to let myself dream even bigger than I had been, I felt a profound gratitude to Saul for his continued generosity to me.

We spent the next few hours organizing our ideas and starting to plan. It was clear Saul and I had very different ideas about what constituted "décor," but still, we were totally aligned with how the building would function. That was amazing.

THE AFTERNOON WAS WONDERFUL, and by the time Lucille picked me up around sunset, I was more relaxed than I had been in months. Somehow, I had managed not to think about work, Sawyer, or the murder/kidnapping in over four hours, and I felt like maybe this was the kind of feeling those meditation masters were always advocating. I made a mental note to meditate more.

Now, though, I had two boys waiting at home for me, and I had just enough time to get there before the youngest one went to bed. When I came into the kitchen, Sawyer jumped up, gave me a hug, and started talking. Apparently it had been story day at school, and Saw had told the class all about his magnifying glass and being a depatee. "But then, I saw Heather was crying, and so I stopped talking." He didn't seem too bothered by this development, but I shot Santiago a puzzled look before telling Sawyer it was time for bed.

"Actually, Mama, Santi and I have a bedtime plan," he said, and for a brief minute, my heart hurt. I loved the idea of Santiago living with us, but I didn't want to be replaced. "You need to put this on," Sawyer continued as he handed me a green and blue bandanna.

"Put this on how?" I said as I studied the fabric in my hands.

"Like this," Santiago said as he took the bandanna, rolled it, and tied it over my eyes like a blindfold. I started to resist and ask my usual boatload of questions, but the little giggle that came from my son's mouth made me pause, be grateful, and let him lead me up the stairs. I said a prayer of gratitude that I only ran into the newel post and one wall on the way and found myself getting pretty excited about what I was going to find upstairs.

First, Sawyer led me into his room, and when Santi took off the blindfold, I gasped. The room was, first of all, immaculate, and second of all, the walls and ceiling were covered in hundreds of glow-in-the-dark stars, comets, and planets. "You added more, Love Bug," I said as I spun around and marveled at the quiet green glow in the room.

"Yep," he said. "Santi brought them for me because I said if we could make my whole room glow, I wanted to sleep in here."

I knelt down and looked at my son. "You do? Does the room glow enough for you to do that?"

He looked around very seriously and then looked me in the eye and said, "As long as you're next door, I can do it." He hugged my legs and then said, "I want to read *Pirate Stew*."

He headed toward his own bed, and I only halted my tears when Santiago said, "Do you want to show your mama her room first?"

"Oh yeah. I almost forgot," Sawyer said as he bolted past me. "Come on."

I followed him out the door and then stopped with awe when he opened mine. There, in the dark, my room glowed like his did. The entire ceiling was covered in colorful, glow-in-the-dark flowers that made it look like a meadow. I couldn't stop the tears this time. "This is beautiful, Sawyer."

"Thanks, Mama. Me and Santi did it for you." Then he walked over to the closet that he and I had covered in drawings. "I'm okay with this being Santi's closet, Mama. Our drawings can just be behind it, okay?"

I sat down on my bed and held out my arms. "That sounds perfect, and maybe we can color in your closet next?" I held my little boy tight against me for longer than he wanted me to do so, but then I said, "Let's all go read *Pirate Stew* in your bed."

Saw sprinted back around the corner and jumped into his bed, which I saw was freshly made and tight as a rubber band. Clearly, Santi had some household skills I was going to appreciate. The three of us clambered into the bed, and Santi and I took turns reading Neil Gaiman's charming book. I was the narrator, and Santi was all the pirates...and it was magical.

Within minutes, Sawyer dozed off, and Santi and I walked back downstairs, only to collapse on the couch ourselves. "I hope it was okay that I talked with him about me moving in. He asked, and I didn't know what to say."

"It's totally fine. He and I had discussed it a bit before, when you'd slept over in his room, but I'm not surprised he asked since he woke up with both of us again this morning." I leaned over and put my head on his shoulder. "That was a lovely way to wake up, by the way."

"I thought so, too," he said as he rested his cheek against my hair. "Not too much."

"Nope, just enough," I said. We sat quietly for a few more minutes, but eventually, both of us got fidgety and started to wiggle. Santiago needed noise, and I needed to do something with my hands. "Let's watch something," I said.

"Only if you sew," he replied as he grabbed the remote.

"Deal," I said as I pulled my sewing basket up from the floor beside the couch. It was remarkably heavy, and it was only when I lifted it to eye height that I could see why. Beauregard was curled up right on top of my fabric. He looked like he'd been there for hours, except now one green eye was open and glaring at me.

"Beau," I said, "this is not a cat bed."

"It is now," Santiago said with a snicker. "He looks mighty comfy."

"Too comfy," I said as I slid my fabric and thread out from under the very furry cat. "If you ruined my project with your fluff..." I held the piece up to the light, and surprisingly, it had very little fur on it. Beauregard was not one to be considerate, but if he had been, I might have thought he groomed himself elsewhere before taking his nap.

Santiago turned on *The Mandalorian*, and for a half-hour I lost myself in my stitches and questions about exactly how does a Yoda that small walk. Does he have knees? Ankles? Or just sort of tube-legs and that he shifts back and forth?

When the episode was over, Santi paused it and looked at me. "You have been so patient. Do you want to know what we found out today?"

I immediately stowed my needle, put the fabric down, and said, "I didn't want to be pushy."

He laughed and patted my hand. "You did very well." Then he leaned back, put his feet in my lap, and said, "My price is that you make good on that promise of a massage that you made yesterday."

Remembering my earlier vow to rub this man's shoulders, I obliged readily and began by stretching his toes as he talked. "So let me start with what Savannah found out about the Foresters. First, Katherine is their only child. They've applied to be foster parents and to adopt, but they've never been accepted for either situation. Too many red flags, is what the social workers told Savannah."

"Thank God that part of the system works, then. It's just too bad we don't have those kinds of checks for biological parents, I guess." I rubbed my thumbs into the arch of Santiago's foot and heard him exhale.

"They are deacons at their church, and she is the book-keeper. He chairs the property committee, and everyone Savannah talked to had glowing things to say but also told her they didn't really know them very well." Santiago leaned his head back and sighed heavily as I rubbed his ankle.

"That's weird, right? I mean I know most of the people at my church, been to a lot of their houses, and I've only been going there for a couple of years. How long have the Foresters been members of theirs?"

Santiago lifted his head and met my eye. "Twenty-two years."

I slid my head back on my neck and picked up his other foot. "That's a long time for people to not really know you."

"Exactly," Santiago said as I began working on his toes. "Everyone just kept saying they 'keep to themselves,' but more than two decades is a long time to be a member of something and still keep to yourself."

I sighed. "I'll say. I didn't make it two weeks at Bethel before I was invited to three dinners and one baptism party." The members of my church were super friendly, and given that I'd started attending with one of their most beloved, my friend Mary, they were very quick to enfold me in their grasp. I was grateful, and I knew not all churches were like that. But that many years and holding key positions at the church without someone being able to talk about you with more than plati-tudes or generalities...something was definitely up.

"Otherwise, it's the same story. They both work – she's a schoolteacher, kindergarten, and he is in middle management at a company down in Charlottesville. Both of their bosses said they were great employees, a little withdrawn but never had complaints. The principal at Mrs. Forester's school said her children did well and she was liked by parents, but she also didn't do much by way of volunteering outside the classroom. Same for Mr. Forester."

"I feel like you're about to tell me they're robots, a la Stepford, or aliens masquerading as middle-class white Americans to infiltrate our society." I took both of Santi's feet in my hands and rubbed them softly.

"No. But witness protection did come to mind for me," he said with a smile.

"And there, sir, is the quintessential difference in the two of us – I go sci-fi/fantasy, and you go police procedural." We both laughed, but then when he sat up, I said, "So what does that mean? Do you think they kidnapped Katherine?"

He shook his head. "No. They wouldn't have raided her campsite like that if they had taken her."

I interrupted. "Do you know it was her parents who raided her camp?"

"Footage from the traffic cam at the bottom of the mountain shows their car headed toward the cabin road late last night. It's not conclusive, but it's pretty close, especially since they live south of town and would really have little reason to go that direction at ten thirty on a Tuesday night." Santiago sounded both disgusted and frustrated. "The thing is, I still don't think they kidnapped her."

"I can see why. I mean, if they were going to try and steal from her, they would have done it before, right? It doesn't seem like they knew where she was." I hadn't really thought through that before, but as soon as I said it, it seemed accurate.

Clearly, Santiago agreed because he said, "Precisely what I was thinking. But they're the only people who have any motive to kidnap her."

"Do they though?" I said. "I mean, she's an adult. And the abuse happened years ago now. Do they really have anything to fear from her at this point?"

Santiago studied my face a minute. "True. But if what they

wanted was in her campsite, then they have a reason to want to find her."

I sighed. "Now, that's she's gone, though... So maybe they could have hired someone?"

A long sigh escaped from his mouth. "Right. So they aren't completely in the clear, but still, I don't have them in mind for the kidnapping."

"Who do you have in mind?" I asked.

"Whoever killed Paul Fletcher." He looked up at the ceiling.

"That's the name of the victim?"

"Yeah. He's not local. From up in Maryland, near Gaithersburg. His friends said he was camping up at Big Meadows last week." Santiago took his notepad out. "They said he came every year at this time, kind of a family tradition from way back, I guess."

Something about the name Fletcher was familiar, so I opened up my laptop and googled him. Nothing came up. I'd have to just keep an eye out for what I was associating with that name. "Mind if I investigate him a little?" I said, completely aware and slightly embarrassed that Santiago had just seen me begin to do just that before I asked his permission.

"Would it do me any good to say, 'No thank you'?" He smirked.

"Of course," I said, but when Santiago gave me a long stare from beneath his eyebrows, I sighed. "Okay, probably not. But I'd rather have your permission."

He laughed. "Sure, do your thing, Pais. Just don't tell anyone but me what you find, okay?"

I nodded and opened all my usual tabs. Within seconds, I was deep into the process, and knowing me well, Santiago kissed the top of my head and went back to watching TV.

Normally when Santi was nearby, I found myself more than a little distracted, but today, maybe because there was now a woman missing as well as a man dead, I found myself very focused. I didn't have much to go on: the dead man's name, his age – which Santi had gotten from his friends, forty-nine – the knowledge that his hometown was in Maryland, and the fact that he had been in the park at least once every year for most of his life.

I started out by searching newspapers, looking for any mention of him that didn't come up on a general search. I hit the jackpot almost immediately: two articles, one from Gaithersburg, and one from a village called Poolesville, just west of there. In each of the articles, Fletcher was lauded as a master metal detectorist. He'd found a number of Civil War buttons and military insignia, but his most important find, the reason for both articles, was that he had, about two years ago, discovered a human arm bone with a gold bracelet still in place. The gold was worth considerable cash, but it was the arm on which it was worn that had been the biggest news item. Apparently, given the location of the find and the quality of the gold, a lot of people wanted to believe the arm bone had belonged to a famous heiress who had become a recluse in antebellum Poolesville.

With that little bit of data, I was off and running, and soon I had a pretty thorough understanding of the excitement around this arm bone. The woman to whom speculation supposed it belonged, Ms. Agatha Granger, had lived in the old Victorian at the edge of Poolesville, and according to legend, she never left the house because she didn't want her twenty-nine cats to think she'd abandoned them. When she'd died, it had taken months for anyone to know, and by the time the neighbors had suggested that the police take a look in her house, the wild animals and her own cats had done a good job of spreading her skeleton to sundry corners of the house.

I shuddered at the thought of Beauregard being left with my corpse. He'd probably do far nastier things to me than Ms. Granger's cats did to her, just out of spite.

I could have gone much further into the Granger legend, I could see that from a cursory search, but my real questions were about Paul Fletcher. Who was he? Why was he in our area every year? And why did someone want him dead?

Once I'd identified him as being from Poolesville, it didn't take me long to build out his family genealogy, and when I got back four generations, I finally landed upon the reason his surname had seemed familiar – his family was one of the others, along with the O'Malleys, that had been forced off their land when the Shenandoah National Park had come through.

I pulled up the list of names used by the Blue Ridge Heritage Project, an organization that had formed in the last twenty years or so to honor and commemorate those families that had been forcefully relocated off the mountains. There they were: Paul's grandparents, Betty and Vincent Fletcher. Their land had been, according to the maps on the site, very close to the O'Malley land. That couldn't be a coincidence.

I spun my laptop toward Santiago and pointed out the names in photos of the historic plaque. He grabbed the remote and paused his episode of *The Mandalorian* on a perfect freeze-frame of Baby Yoda doing his magical Jedi stuff.

"Well, how about them apples?" Santi said as he studied the screen. "Can you tell if Paul Fletcher's ancestors were there at the same time as the O'Malleys?"

I pulled up the 1930 census, the last one before the national park was established, and sure enough, the Fletchers and the O'Malleys were listed next to each other on the census. "Looks like it," I said as I showed Santi the screen again. "I can't be absolutely certain, but usually census takers went house by house in order."

He nodded. "Looks like I need to talk to Frank O'Malley again."

I sighed. Frank and Nancy had been through a lot this week already, and I hated that Santi had to follow this lead. But I knew he needed to, and I also knew that Frank and Nancy would understand. Still, I couldn't help offering a suggestion. "What if you talked to Frank's cousin Patrick first?"

Santiago looked up at the ceiling and then over at me. "You know I love that you want to protect your friends, don't you?"

I snuggled closer to him. "I didn't know that specifically, but I like it. So what do you think? Patrick first?"

He wrapped an arm around me and pushed the top of my laptop closed. "Sure, Pais. I can do that." He kissed my cheek. "Now, more Baby Yoda."

I smiled and put my head on his chest. Baby Yoda sounded perfect.

7

The next morning after we dropped Sawyer off at school, and after learning that Saul didn't need me at the shop site, we headed out to see Patrick O'Malley. Santiago had decided it might grease the wheels of information a bit if I went along to talk about family history and the cabin. It was all relevant to the case, especially given the new information about the Fletchers we'd found the night before, but Patrick didn't need to know that.

Patrick was a middle-aged bachelor who owned a gorgeous house tucked into a little valley just north of Charlottesville. I wasn't sure exactly what someone did to be able to afford this kind of luxury at our age, but I was eager to find out.

When we pulled up to the stone-faced house, we saw a man with dark hair walking through a nearby pasture with a trail of longhorn cattle coming behind him. From where we stood, we could hear him talking to the animals in the sort of conversational tone I adopted with Beauregard when he and I were home alone together. Companionship without response was sometimes the best thing – at least, that's the reason I owned a cat.

When Patrick caught sight of us, he threw up a hand and smiled wide. "Someone isn't bothered by a visit from the police," I remarked quietly as I waved back.

"Not yet," Santi said as he moved toward our host. "Nice cattle!"

"Thanks. Just a hobby for me, but I love these girls. They're like pets." He reached back and scratched a red forehead. "Want to say hi?"

I never refuse a chance to meet an animal, so I climbed up the wooden fence, leaned over, and was greeted by a half-dozen fuzzy heads and wet noses. It took me a minute to realize they were experts at dodging things with their long horns, and initially, I was ducking every two seconds.

Eventually, though, we had a grand old time greeting one another, and Santiago even got in on the action, although he has a much more "old-school" sense of animals' places. Given how much cuddle time he gave Beau, though, I expected I was wearing him down.

Cattle greetings over, Patrick invited us into the house and casually pointed out the boot scraper by the side door. I had been meaning to get one of these for Sawyer and me, more for our stream adventures and puddle jumping that involved mud than for cow manure, but when I saw how effectively it cleaned up all our shoes, I put it high on my "to find" list.

Inside, my list of "to find" quickly filled up with dream items: a vintage farmhouse sink, soapstone countertops, a primitive dresser that was doubling as a kitchen desk. The kitchen alone must have been 900 square feet, and I was having a hard time not feeling envious, even though I loved my quaint little kitchen.

Patrick pointed out the washroom just off the hall from the kitchen, and while each of us took turns removing the scented gifts of the cattle, Patrick directed the other to the Keurig in the corner and his cabinet full of pods with everything from assorted teas to dark roast coffee to my choice, a K-cup with what appeared to be the exact same sickly sweet fake cappuccino I'd consumed by the case in college. Sure enough, as soon as I tasted my first sip, I could have been at my desk with my Brother word processor typing up a paper for Modern Brit Lit.

It didn't take me long to return to the here and now, though, because as Patrick led us to a small, glass-roofed conservatory off the kitchen, I spotted what looked like muddy hiking poles and boots next to the door that led, I assumed, to the garage. I shot Santiago a look with a nod over my head, and he nodded back. He'd seen them, too.

We sat down at a round table, and I took a long gaze out the window into the forest and fields below the house. I could see all the way to the winding road we'd come in on, and with the mountains surrounding us on all sides, I felt like I was in one of the protected glens of the elves from The Lord of the Rings. This sense was reinforced by the fact that the glass-sided room was full of house plants and citrus trees, and the air in the space was humid, warm, and scented like the earth.

I had about a thousand compliments I wanted to pay Patrick on his house and its setting, but the image of those boots and the poles had grounded me, pun intended, in a very real sense. They could just be the remains of a hiking expedition from another time, but this situation around Fletcher's murder and Forester's disappearance was beginning to be a bit too full of coincidences to seem natural.

Fortunately, Santiago and I were on the same wavelength because he didn't waste any time getting to the heart of our visit. "Mr. O'Malley, I don't know whether you have heard or not, but the body of a man named Paul Fletcher was recently found in your family's cabin up near the Parkway."

For a split second, something that looked like anger flashed across Patrick's face, but then his expression settled into one of surprise. "No, I hadn't heard that. When? And why was Paul's body in our cabin?"

My thoughts pulled up short when he referred to the victim by first name, but I held my tongue.

"Last week," Santi said, "on the day the cabin was scheduled to be disassembled by Ms. Sutton and her team." He studied Patrick's face for a minute. "Did you know the victim?"

I suppressed my smile as I recognized Santi's usual interrogation tactic – give them a little information and then follow up with a question.

Patrick paused and took a long sip from his mug. Then, he met Santiago's gaze and said, "Yes, I did. Paul and I used to date some time ago." He reached into his wallet and took out an old picture from the first era when mullets were in fashion. Egads.

If I had been surprised before, I was really surprised now. "Was it serious?" I asked before I could help myself.

Patrick nodded. "We were together for ten years." His face grew sad, and he looked around his house. "This house was our dream together." He looked down at the mug in his hands. "But Paul didn't want to live in a rural space, and I really did...and eventually, that difference drove us apart."

"How long ago was that?" Santi asked.

"Seven years," Patrick said, "when he got a job up in Northern Virginia. My work is in Charlottesville, and I had this plot of land. It seemed like a natural time to let things go." His face was creased with sadness as he turned his gaze out the window. "I hadn't talked to him in a few months, but we did keep in touch a little."

Santiago sighed. "I'm sorry for your loss, and forgive my questions. But I have to ask, did Paul know about your cabin?"

This time Patrick didn't hesitate. "Of course. We went up there often when we were first together. His family had owned land next to it, and like us, they were displaced for the park. His family's place had long ago fallen in, but we enjoyed the sense of deep roots when we spent weekends at the cabin." A small smile played across his lips. "Those were good days."

Santiago made a note that I could just read over his shoulder. *Both men knew cabin.*

"Did you know I was taking the cabin down?" I asked as Santiago continued to write what I could now see were simply a bunch of squiggly lines. Clearly, he had a strategy here, so I hoped he didn't mind when I stepped in.

"Frank told me, and I can't say I was thrilled. Only, though, because I wished we could get the funds together to save it." He sighed. "But I was the only one invested in that idea, so I figured it was better for the wood to be saved than for the forest to get it back." He met my eyes then. "I've heard you're really good at your job, and that you spend a lot of time gathering history and then sharing the stories. Anything you know yet?"

I shook my head. "Nothing that you don't already know, it seems. Since I didn't know that you and Fletcher were well acquainted, I had come today to give you the information about your family properties, but you're well aware of that." I watched as Patrick nodded.

"You did do some work on Patrick's family, though, right?" Santiago said with a firm stare.

I took the hint. "I did." I pulled two sheets of folded paper out of my coat pocket and opened them up before spinning them to face Patrick. "This is your family tree going back to Ireland."

Patrick leaned down to study the small type on the paper. "How did you get all this information?"

"It's just what Paisley does, Mr. O'Malley. Did you know this part of your family history?"

He shook his head. "No. As far as I know, none of us know this. Our grandparents just didn't talk about the past much, and given that they were third generation over here, maybe they didn't know much to talk about." Patrick looked up at me again. "Thank you for this. I can't wait to tell my cousins."

"Well, Frank already knows," I said and felt a hard shove against my foot under the table. I scrambled to recover and figure out why Santi wouldn't want me to share that information. "Or at least I think he knows. I sent him the same trees as you have here."

"Good," Patrick said. "Then we can talk about it, maybe over a nice bottle of Irish whiskey. Toast the old family, you know?" His voice dropped into the same kind of lilt I had heard in Frank's voice a few days before. Clearly, the Irish brogue had been passed down in some way.

I smiled. "I hope it will give you joy to know more about your history. You might want to look at some books about the building of the Blue Ridge Tunnel down in Afton. I think your ancestors might have worked on it. Mary Lyons has a couple of good ones." I had every intention of looking at those books myself to see what else I could learn both about the Fletchers and the O'Malleys, but since they were public record and I subscribed to Santiago's give-goodwill-to-get-good-info method, I figured it couldn't hurt to share that information.

Patrick grabbed a pen from where it sat next to a journal on a nearby table. "Mary Lyons you said? Thanks." He jotted her name on the top of the sheets of paper I'd given him. "Now, do you mind if I ask a couple of questions?"

Santiago nodded. "I'll tell you what I can."

"Why was Paul's body in our cabin?" His voice had taken on a bit of a cutting edge, and I was surprised by the quick change in tone from his lilting curiosity just seconds before.

Santi shook his head. "We don't know. That's something we'd like to figure out too. Any guesses?" He looked up, in what I knew was a false casualness, from his notebook. "Any theories?"

Patrick looked out the windows at the pastures again. "Not a

one. You're sure he just didn't die there of exposure or something?" He glanced back at the sheriff.

"The gunshot wound to the back leads us to believe it was
murder," Santiago said, this time with complete seriousness.

I stared at my boyfriend. This was the first I'd heard of
cause of death, and it was a doozy. Shot in the back. There's
nothing accidental or withdrawn about that. I shivered.

"Well, I suppose not," Patrick said as he turned his gaze
back to Santiago. "Was he killed there?"

Santiago's jaw clenched, but he kept the rest of his face
neutral. "We don't believe so." Santi broke his attention from
Patrick's face and doodled on his notepad again. "Why do you
ask that?"

I was very curious to hear this answer myself, and I watched
Patrick's face as I waited for his answer.

A slight flush ran up his neck, reminding me of his cousin
Frank. "I'm actually not sure. Something about the way you
said you found his body there made me think, I guess, he might
have died somewhere else." He shrugged, but even I could tell
he was trying to cover something up. My opinion of Patrick
O'Malley had taken on a darker hue since we'd arrived.

Santiago stood up, and I scrambled to my feet after him.
"Thank you for your time, Mr. O'Malley. You'll let me know if
you think of anything about Paul I might need to know?" He
handed Patrick a business card.

"Of course," Patrick said as he led us through a large great
room to the front door this time. "Nice to meet you both." The
casual friendliness was back in his voice.

"Oh, I almost forgot to ask," Santi said as we stepped onto
the small stoop outside. "What kind of car do you drive?"

Patrick glanced toward the garage. "A Dodge Ram." He met
Santi's gaze. "You looking for a particular car?"

Santi lied without a hitch in his step. "Nope. Just routine
information in case we get any leads on a vehicle."

I waved to Patrick and then to the cattle as I sat back into the front seat of Santiago's cruiser. We turned around on the wide pavers in front of the garage and headed back out the drive. As soon as we turned onto the road, I said, "That was weird. He didn't even seem surprised that Paul Fletcher was dead."

"No, no he did not," Santiago said. "Not even a little."

FOR THE REST of the ride up through the mountains and back to my shop, we were quiet. I was trying to think through all the reasons why Patrick O'Malley might have known his ex-boyfriend was dead, and I didn't even want to speculate about what Santiago was thinking. His face was stern, and while he drove carefully all the way, he definitely was tending some aggression by taking the curves a bit faster than usual.

When he put the car in park in front of the nearly-complete two-story house on Saul's lot, I gave Santiago a quick kiss on the cheek and opened the door. He was clearly deep in thought, and I didn't want to interrupt his processing. I hated when I couldn't think through something thoroughly, and since I rarely had time to do that these days, I honored that need in people a great deal.

I walked around the back of the car and was almost to the front door of the house when Santiago said my name. "Pais, be careful, okay? Something isn't coming together about all this yet, but I have a feeling that we're poking the bear."

"I hear you, and I'll be careful. I'll get Saul to run me home in a bit, and I'll keep you posted about where Saw and I are." I leaned over. "I'll keep my eyes open."

"Blue Dodge Durango," he said after I gave him a little kiss. "If you see it..."

"You'll be the first person to know." I smiled and tried to look confident as I walked into the shell of the house before me. But I couldn't shake the feeling that Santiago was right. Something was very wrong here in Octonia.

Saul was just inside the door, overseeing the placement of the rafters, when I walked in, and I was glad for the distraction. The house was much larger than I remembered, and the interior walls were made up of rough-hewn logs that, now that Saul's crew had cleaned them up, gave the building a rustic but lived-in feeling. It was gorgeous.

"Wow, Saul. You guys know how to build a house," I said as I slid my fingers over the logs in what would soon be my office. "Are we thinking we'll leave the wood bare?"

"I think so, Paisley-girl. It's too pretty to cover up, don't you think?" He walked over and pointed. "If it suits you, we'll just chink the logs and keep it simple. That way, people can see the beauty of the structure—"

"And if we ever need to sell it, takedown is simpler," I finished.

"That's right. I don't see that happening, since I sold another lot of your boards today while you were gone, but you never know." He gestured out the frame of the window to where a large collection of old barnwood had sat just this morning. "Fellow from out in Harrisonburg bought it up. Going to use it for his office."

Saul told me what the guy paid for the wood I'd gotten for only the cost of the labor needed to take down the old tobacco barn, and I had to work hard to keep from clapping my hands and squealing with glee. "Wow, thanks, Saul. That'll be a good chunk of change to put toward the windows and things we need here."

"I figured you'd be pleased, and the window guys are coming later today. We'll have the roof on by then, and I figured we'd get them working ASAP so we could cool this place down." Saul sauntered over to the central hall, where two members of his crew were already building a staircase with what looked to be some of my other salvaged wood. "Took that small lot you had to do this. Save us a little money."

"Perfect," I said, almost as glad for the savings as I was for the income. My dad had taught me that a penny saved is a penny earned, and given that windows and rugs and all the furniture we were going to need for my office and to display my wares well were going to cost a pretty penny, I was glad for every bit I didn't need to spend. Besides the stairs were going to be gorgeous, especially when we stained the old ash boards to a dark red. I could already picture the arrangement of old hardware spanning the long wall to the second story.

I spent the next few hours on my laptop pricing vintage furniture and scoping out rugs and window coverings. I wasn't much of a decorator, but it was fun to think about the aesthetic of the rooms and how we would make them cozy without overpowering the building or the things I had for sale. I had in mind a color scheme based in orange, blue, green, and touches of pink, and I figured we could do a feature wall of one color in each of the upstairs rooms to provide some visual contrast from all the wood and metal that made up most of what I had for sale.

Of course, I'd let Saul decorate his own space, within reason. His current desk was made up of sawhorses and a piece of plywood, so we were going to have to go a little more formal than that. But I had a primitive dining table in mind that I thought might double as a desk and conference table and not feel too "fancy schmancy," as he would say. If I went with simple cream curtains on all the downstairs windows, I figured he'd tolerate that, too, and it would make the space look unified from the outside.

The window guys arrived around two, and Saul and I walked around with them as they measured the not-at-all standard windows. It was going to be a big job to have them put in, but we decided to go whole hog and have them make the glass wavy, like it was handmade, and also have them use muntins to give it the old-world look. They could even do it in a gray-brown color that would match the patina of the logs.

By the time we were done, my heart was racing with anxiety over the cost of all this, and I was strategizing ways to make some fast cash to cover my expenses. I was doing well, what with the market on the weekends and the growing customer base for my larger lots, but without the O'Malley cabin, I was going to have to find some additional funds to pay for all of this and still be able to pay myself. Given that both Sawyer and I required housing and food, I had to find some more money, and fast.

Saul went to gather his things before he took me home, and I sat down with my notebook and pen to do the actual financials on paper. I was staring at the total figure for all these improvements when Saul's shadow shaded my paper. "It's going to be a big endeavor," he said, "but it's a good tax write-off."

I looked up at his face, and he was grinning ear to ear. "That is good," I said, trying to sound more hopeful than I felt. The tax refund would be nice come spring of next year, but the money to pay for things now was a more pressing concern.

"Oh, and did I mention that I'm covering all the expenses now that you're going to be paying rent?" Saul sounded so casual that I thought I might have misheard him.

"Excuse me?"

"You heard me, missy. I'm covering this. You'll pay me rent on the space, and we'll both come out ahead. I get security and more of a presence at my lot, and you get some display space." He started walking toward his truck that was parked near the front gate. "You coming?"

I stared at his back for a while and then got up, suddenly feeling like skipping. I hadn't always been good at accepting help, and I was still very bad at asking for it. But over the past couple of years, since Sawyer's dad and I divorced and I started my own business, I'd learned that when the people who cared about me offered to support me, I needed to take that support, pride be damned.

I didn't take it for granted though, and when I closed the door on Saul's truck, I leaned over and gave him a quick hug. "Thank you, Saul," I whispered.

"Don't thank me yet, Paisley-girl. You haven't seen what I have in mind for decor yet." He laughed and pulled out of the gate.

8

After Saul dropped me at my house, I bolted at the speed of light to get the house a little tidier – and Beauregard a little less grumpy – before I had to go pick up Sawyer. I had thought about asking Saul if we could grab him on the way home, but then I'd hit upon an adventure for Sawyer and me that would let us get out a bit and help me with my research, too.

I'd always envied those parents whose children ran toward them when they'd been parted for a time, but I hadn't had much experience in that particular joy. Sawyer had always been the kind who clung back, holding on to the person they'd just been with. Today, though, when I pulled up to the school and Sawyer saw me, he sprinted across the schoolyard and leapt into my arms. I barely kept my balance as he scrambled up my body like a little monkey and wrapped his arms around my throat. "I love you so much, Mama."

My breath shortened, both from tears and from the tightness of his hug, but I managed, "I love you, too."

He pulled back, put his hands on my cheeks and said, "You're supposed to say, 'I love you, too, Sawyer.'"

I studied his intent expression and then said, "I love you, too, Sawyer."

Satisfied, he slid to the ground and took my hand. "Let's go home," he said.

"Actually, I wondered if you wanted to take an adventure," I said as I buckled him into his car seat. "We have just enough time to get up to the Parkway for a picnic and the sunset. And I brought chocolate." I waved an orange bag of his favorite candies in front of him. "What do you say?"

He put one finger to his cheek and tapped, considering. "Let's do it," he said.

I smiled, handed him a pouch of apple juice, and climbed into the front seat. "Off we go," I said with a grin in the rearview mirror.

He gave me a thumbs-up and then settled into his own quiet space. I was eager to hear about his day, but he needed the quiet, I could tell. I figured I'd hear about his day on our picnic.

But before we got to one of the picnic areas, I wanted to head south to see how the land lay, now that I'd studied the maps of the area a bit more closely. I'd learned in my months of doing this work that this kind of hands-on – or tires-on – experience was irreplaceable, and while I'd walked around this mountainside a couple of times this week, I hadn't done so with my mind toward property lines and trade routes.

One of the older maps had shown that the logging road that now intersected the Parkway – and that had, apparently, given our killer access to the O'Malley cabin – had once been a wagon road over the mountain to a little community called Beldor. From there, traders would have been able to head down to Elkton and Waynesboro or further west, even, to Crozet. I didn't know what good it would do me to see those old road traces with that in mind, but I figured it couldn't hurt. And the chance to be with Sawyer on the Parkway at sunset, well, that was something I wasn't going to miss out on.

We pulled off at the overlook where we'd found the note from Katherine Forester, and Saw and I both stepped out and carefully crossed the road. There, just visible through the ever-growing forest, I could make out what had once been a road-way. I only recognized it because it looked like what my friends in the desert states called an *arroyo*. If someone didn't know better, they might think it was a former creek bed. But the evenly spaced ruts running down the middle combined with the trees a foot or so higher on either side of the roadbed told me this had once been the wagon road. I took Sawyer's hand, and we jumped the few feet to the hillside below. He landed with ease. I thought my ankles were going to break, but we were down and walking.

"I like this adventure, Mama," he said as he scampered ahead. "We're bushtapping."

I laughed. "I think you mean bushwhacking, and sort of. But we're not going to break anything or pull up any plants. This is a national park, and we protect everything here." I followed behind him until he got to the roadbed, and then he stopped. "Look Mama, a road," he said and pointed down the hillside.

"That's my boy," I said. "Sure is. Wagons used to use this road." I stared down the mountain to where I could just see the tops of a few houses where the elevation leveled off a little. I wouldn't really want to walk down this roadway, much less take a wagon down it. But then, I wasn't a frontierswoman.

Sawyer interrupted my reflection when he said, "Look, Mama, a ring," and held up what I expected to be a soda tab. But sure enough, it was an actual ring with a small red stone in it. "Can I keep it?"

I started to say yes, but then I caught the glimmer of light on something a bit further down the road. "Come see what this is with me, Saw." We jogged down the old road, and he bent to pick up a AAA battery.

"Someone littered," he said with a scowl.

I nodded and said, "Yes, someone did. We'll take that home and recycle it. Why don't you put it in your pocket with the ring?"

He grinned and carefully opened his front right pocket to slide his new treasures inside. As he did, I noticed something rising from the trees down the hill. Normally, I didn't rely on my preschooler for his understanding of the world yet, but if I was seeing what I thought I was seeing, Sawyer would recognize it right away.

"Saw, do you see that above the trees?"

He looked where I pointed and then said, "Smoke!" He sniffed the air. "There's a fire, Mama. We need to call the fire department."

I pulled him to me quickly and leaned close to his ear. "It's not a big fire," I whispered. "But someone has lit a campfire, which is illegal. Maybe someone is hurt or lost, so let's go see."

"We can help," he said far too loudly for the way my nerves were jangling.

"Maybe we can, Love Bug," I whispered as I took his hand. "But we need to be very quiet. It's possible these are bad guys, and we don't want them to see us if that's the case."

I really hated playing into this overly simplistic idea of "good guys" and "bad guys," but in this case, something was telling me that we might not want to be seen. And the only way I could think to communicate that clearly to my son was with that stereotype.

Given that I had enough intuition to know it might be good to stay unnoticed, it might be reasonable to think my intuition should have just told me to go back to the car and call Santiago. But my intuition wasn't always consistent, while my curiosity usually was.

Sawyer and I literally tiptoed down the hill to the edge of the road parallel to where we'd seen the smoke. There, in the woods, I saw a green canvas tent, kind of like the one I'd once bought on Craigslist and found it took six people and two hours to put up. It was sturdy and waterproof, but not light-weight. Not, in other words, something people set up for a casual camping trip.

Given that the sun was close to setting and we were now on the western side of the mountain, the sunlight was sort of like a spotlight on the small campsite. Beside the tent, I saw a firepit made from rocks and a clothesline hung with at least two sets of clothes, one larger than the other.

Sawyer kept pointing up the mountain and trying to drag me back up the trail toward our car, but I wanted to get a closer look. I had started to step into the woods when Sawyer shouted, "Mama, run!" He was looking down the mountain now, and it was only then that I heard what he had probably picked up much earlier than I had, given his young ears. A UTV was coming up the road toward us.

Saw and I sprinted up the road, and with a strength I didn't have, I scooped him up and tossed him into a thick stand of ferns a few dozen yards above the campsite. I could only hope that whoever was on that UTV hadn't seen us and that the sound of the machine had covered our noisy attempt to hide.

I looked down at Sawyer and put my finger to his lips. He nodded, and with eyes as wide as saucers, he sank down into the plants. I followed suit and said a silent prayer of thanks that we were both dressed in mostly dark blue today. If Saw had been wearing his bright-orange, "Fun In the Mud" shirt we could have been in real trouble.

When the UTV cut off down the hill from us, I let out a slow sigh of relief. Surely if they had seen us, they would have come on up this way. But just because they hadn't seen us didn't mean they wouldn't. After all, we couldn't crouch in the woods all night. Santiago was due to meet us in an hour and a half, and while he knew we were on the Parkway, I hadn't exactly told him we were coming down this way to check out this old roadbed.

As we hid, I heard the voices of one man and one woman talking, and while I didn't think they were whispering, they certainly weren't projecting their voices for our benefit, either. A moment or two later, I heard grunting and stuck my head up just enough to see them pushing the UTV off the roadbed and into the woods. Clearly, they knew how to cover their tracks. In fact, I was surprised to think they had left a fire burning in daylight like that.

That surprise was something our UTV friends shared, apparently, because a moment later, I heard the woman yell, "Put that out. Someone will see it." Then, the clear hiss of water on flame skirted up the mountain.

Sawyer looked at me, and while he was doing an amazing job of being quiet, I knew his nerves were getting to him by the way he was beginning to fidget. The boy couldn't stay still on a calm, good day after a dose of Benadryl. He wasn't going to last long in this situation. We had to get out of here.

I risked poking my head out of the ferns one more time and scanned the hillside like my head was a periscope. The ferns continued up the mountainside a good ways, almost to the overlook it seemed. If we stayed off the roadbed and were quiet, I thought we could get back to our car without being seen.

Sawyer was not yet old enough to watch movies with soldiers, but I hoped the signals I'd picked up from my own film experience might communicate well to a little boy. I put my fingers to my lips, pointed up the hill, and then walked two fingers across the air like I was tiptoeing.

He nodded, and then I took his hand and began to climb, slowly and quietly, doing my best to step over twigs and branches to avoid giving away our location. Sawyer did brilliantly, and given that he weighed a lot less than me, he made far less sound. I was very proud of him.

We were almost to the stone barrier that made up the overlook when I got careless and misplaced my foot on a slick pile of leaves. I went flailing down the hill. Only mother's instinct allowed me to let go of Sawyer's hand so I didn't pull him with me. I yelled as I hit a hard limb about ten feet down the hill, and while I got very quiet very quickly, I heard the sound of shouting and footsteps coming from the camp.

"Run!" I shouted to Sawyer as I extricated myself from the branches of a fallen pine and hauled after him through the plants.

Sawyer had watched Lucille climb the cliffs of the North Mountain enough times to be a skilled rock climber, and by the time I reached the overlook wall, he was already at the top. I couldn't climb it though, so I said, "I'll meet you around there," and pointed north. Then, I took off running the few feet to the edge of the overlook where I scrambled up the steep slope with the help of adrenaline.

There, Saw was waiting, and while he looked terrified, he was also focused. "They're coming, Mama. Run!"

He and I both sprinted toward our car and got in just in time to see a red-headed woman and a burly white guy with a full brown beard come up the slope that I'd just crossed. As I spun the wheel and did a donut in the parking lot to get going back north on the Parkway, they watched us.

I had my hand on Sawyer in the front seat, a feeble attempt to keep him safe until I could get us out of there, but I took just enough time to look at the couple as we drove by. The woman looked familiar somehow, but in that moment, I didn't have enough brain cells firing with anything but fear to know why.

. . .

DESPITE THE FACT that Sawyer was riding free in the car, I didn't stop until we got all the way down the mountain. There, I pulled into the pottery shop, strapped Sawyer in, and called Santiago. He answered on the first ring, and when I told him what we'd seen, he said he'd send Savannah right up and that I needed to come to the station to give a statement. "I'll call the rangers, too. Maybe they can get there before the couple packs up."

I hadn't thought of that when I decided to get pretty far away before stopping, but given that I'd put my son in danger once already, I figured it was best to get him to safety – at least the relative safety of my car without his car seat – before stopping. Now, I wondered if I'd made the right decision.

As we drove the rest of the way into town, Sawyer talked nonstop about the bad guys and the quick getaway and about how he'd been on the "big road" without his seat belt. Clearly, the fear was wearing off, and now, this was going to be a story of great adventure. I smiled as he talked and hoped that was all it would be, and not also a story of the time his mother almost got him killed.

Once I pulled into the parking lot behind the station, my own nerves had calmed, and I was able to think a bit more clearly about what we'd seen. Maybe it was just someone camping illegally in the park. Maybe they were down on their luck and making do. Maybe they had a pot operation up there, and while that wasn't exactly a safe situation to walk up on, it wasn't something I hadn't dealt with in the past, surprisingly enough.

Unfortunately, I didn't think any of those things was actually the case. We had already piled up a list of events that made *coincidence* seem like a magical phrase. The odds that a random couple were secretly hiding in the national park just up the literal road from where a woman had been kidnapped and a body dumped were so astronomical that I couldn't even imagine the figure.

Santiago met us at the front door when we walked in, and Sawyer leapt into his arms, saying, "We found a secret campsite, and we evaded capture."

I stared at my verbally precocious kid and said, "Where in the world did you hear the phrase 'evaded capture'?" I glanced at Santi to give him a wide-eyed stare and noticed that he was bright red. "You taught him that phrase?"

"We were playing LEGO people, and it just came up," the sheriff said with a sheepish grin. "On the up side, he used it correctly."

I sighed. "He did." A yawn escaped my lips, and I suddenly felt the exhaustion that comes after an adrenaline rush.

"Come sit down in my office," Santi said as he shifted Saw to one hip and came to my side to put his other arm around me. He kissed my cheek and said, "You know, it's usually the partner of the police officer that has to worry about their safety, not the officer worrying about his love."

"I've never been one for traditional roles," I said as I stifled another yawn. Then, I slumped into the chair in front of Santi's desk and wrapped myself around Sawyer when he lumbered into my lap, yawning himself. "Okay, so you want an official statement."

"I do, and I know you're tired, but it's important to get this down when it's fresh in your mind." He smiled and took out his notebook.

I narrated the tale of our time in the wood, including every detail I could recall. Saw helpfully remembered that the clothes on the line were mostly green, and he also said the woman who had chased us had on hiking boots like his dad's. That detail was very specific because his dad only wore Merrell boots. It was a key fact.

When we finished our story, Santiago looked at each of us and said, "Anything else? Anything else at all?"

Sawyer buried his face in my chest in the telltale gesture of a child with something to hide. I lifted his face so his eyes met mine. "You need to tell Santi what you remember, Love Bug."

He let out a long sigh. "Okay." It was only when he reached down and opened his front pocket that I remembered the ring and the battery he'd found. He set them both on the table and then told Santiago we'd found them on the road above the campsite.

"Thank you for telling me, Sawyer," Santi said as he carefully used a pencil to pick up the ring. "And this was just on the roadway?" He put it close to his eye. "It looks like a ruby. Whoever lost this is probably quite upset."

"A ruby?!" Sawyer said as if he was the world's foremost gemologist. The boy had never seen or heard of a ruby before, of that I was sure.

"I'll have to be sure, but it looks like it." Santi poked the battery with his pencil. "What have you all seen AAA batteries in? I'm thinking remote controls, maybe toys."

I shook my head. "That's all we use them for in our house."

"Maybe someone's RC car or something?" Santi said as he pulled an evidence bag out of his desk. "We'll check it out." He looked up at Sawyer. "These could be good clues, Saw. Good work."

I had my doubts that these objects had anything to do with this situation, but I appreciated that Santiago gave my boy a little boost.

But now, I could hear my own stomach growling, and if I was hungry, Sawyer was about three seconds from a total meltdown. "Time for us to get some food," I said.

Santiago nodded. "I'm picking up a pizza. Meet you at the house?"

I noticed he didn't say *your* house or *our* house. We were in that weird in-between, but I just knew we'd find our way.

Not tonight, though. Tonight I just needed food and bed...with maybe a few stitches in between.

THE PIZZA WAS PERFECT, and the soda Santi got to go with it tasted so good. Sugar after stress was just perfect, and even with the extra jolt of sucrose, Sawyer was almost asleep in his plate. And when I took him up to bed, he was out before I even finished reading one book.

When I came down, Santi was stretched all the way across the couch and lifted his feet when he saw me, so I could slide under. He didn't even bother turning on the TV.

I picked up my sewing and began to stitch a little of another branch of the tree while the silence of my house eased out the last of the day's tension. Between the motion of my stitches and Santi's deep breaths, I found myself in that space that was almost, but not quite, sleep.

When my cloth fell into my lap, I gave up and let my eyes close. I was just about asleep when I remembered the picture of Katherine Forester and the O'Malleys. I sat bolt upright.

"That ring – it's Katherine Forester's," I almost shouted.

9

Unfortunately, my near-sleep revelation meant Santi and I didn't get to sleep for a couple more hours. He called the O'Malleys and confirmed that Katherine did indeed have a ring like the one we'd found, and then he checked in with the ranger and Savannah to see if they'd had any luck at the campsite Sawyer and I had found.

As he expected, the campsite had been abandoned by the time they reached it, and so they hadn't bothered to call him, figuring bad news could wait until morning. Since Savannah was working the overnight shift, she had planned to see what she could uncover from the various belongings the couple had left behind, and so far, she could confirm that there were actually three people at the site. Santiago said she'd found two sizes of women's clothes and a pile of men's clothing, too.

"The other woman must have been the one burning the fire," I said when he relayed his conversation as we sat with cups of hot tea on my front porch. "Do you think it was Katherine Forester?"

"Seems unlikely," he said, "since they probably wouldn't leave their victim unattended." He paused and looked out over the field below us. "But who knows? This case gets weirder and weirder."

I couldn't disagree with him there. "I keep meaning to ask you, any leads on the blue Durango?"

Santi shook his head. "Nothing definitive. Still chasing down names."

I understood what Santi had meant about the kidnappers not leaving Katherine to her own devices, but somehow I just couldn't get it out of my mind that she could have been right there and we hadn't saved her. The guilt felt like a lead weight in my chest.

Still, the day had been long and tiring, and when Santiago suggested we go to bed, I didn't object. Citing his need for extra comfort that night, he carried Beauregard upstairs with us and laid him carefully on a chenille blanket at Sawyer's feet.

I kissed Santi goodnight and climbed into my side of the bed, wrapping the blankets carefully around my head. I figured it would be a good hour before I calmed enough to sleep, but the chamomile and conversation must have worked their magic because the next thing I knew, it was 7:30 in the morning.

I'd barely moved all night, and I was glad I had my back to the boys because I had drooled like a champion overnight. Talk about a good night's sleep.

The guys were both still snoozing away, and while I knew that Santi would want to wake and head to work soon, I couldn't manage to make myself wake him when he was snuggled with Sawyer and both of them were sleeping so soundly. Plus, I kind of loved the idea of having my cup of coffee alone that morning. I needed a little chance to think, and the fact that I might be able to make it through my email uninterrupted felt like no small luxury.

I slipped downstairs and made the coffee. While the kettle boiled, I opened my email and scanned the long list of messages that had come in overnight. Most were advertisements that I vowed, once again, to unsubscribe from. One, though, was a query about an item I had for sale on my website, and two were responses to my newsletter.

I replied to the query first because, well, I had a business to run and this woman wanted to buy my entire collection of crystal doorknobs for use as a signature item in her interior designs. I gave her a quote for a ten percent discount on the lot and hoped that would cinch the deal that would cover my rent at Saul's for this month and next.

Then, I turned to the newsletter responses. The first was a note about a message I sent out a few weeks earlier to ask if folks would let me know if they heard about old buildings that someone needed help taking down. My neighbor from up the road had an old chicken coop that she wanted gone so that she could put in a pool. She offered to let me keep anything I found in exchange for the labor. That was my kind of deal, so I replied right away to let her know I'd be in touch with dates as soon as possible.

The final message came from what looked like a fake email address. Since the subject line included my newsletter title, I clicked it open anyway. I scanned the short note and then immediately went upstairs to wake Santi. The sender wrote that they had information about the body at the "O'Malley place" and asked if I was interested in learning what they knew. They also said, *No police*, but I wasn't very well going to follow that directive.

Before his eyes were even open all the way, Santiago was on the phone to Savannah with a request to track down the emailer's information. "I need you to reply," he said. "Tell them you'd like to meet to talk."

I nodded and started to answer.

"No, wait until I'm gone. Give me a chance to get the cruiser out of your driveway just in case."

I started to object, to say that this person surely wouldn't know the sheriff had spent the night at my house, but then I remembered the previous times when people had threatened me at my home and kept my mouth shut. Santiago chugged a cup of coffee, took the printout of the email I gave him, and told me he'd talk to me soon before kissing my cheek and heading out the door. I didn't even have a chance to tell him that his hair was sticking up in the back before he was off at a jog to his cruiser.

Sawyer was still sleeping when I snuck up to check on him again, so I had a little time to write my email response. I kept it short but direct:

I'd love to know what you have to share. I won't call the police before we meet, but I can't make any promises for after. Where and when?

It wasn't technically a lie about calling the police since I'd just whispered to the sheriff, and I figured a white lie for a good cause was worth it.

The sender's reply came almost immediately.

Today. 11 a.m. Coffee shop on Main. I'll be wearing a purple flower.

In the back of my mind, the *Mission: Impossible* theme song started playing, and I imagined myself sliding into a table with my double shot Americano and pistachio biscotti only to hear someone say, "the pig flies at noon" from the table behind me. I'd turn to see a folded newspaper left on the table but not a person in sight. There, inside the sports page, a note would tell me what the informant wanted me to know.

In reality, the meetup was much more pedestrian and involved a woman who looked like she'd just left a DAR meeting, two vanilla lattes, and a window-side table. The informant, a one Mrs. William T. Weatherby, as she introduced herself, was what I could only describe as adorable. She had a purple dahlia brooch on her lapel, wore her silver hair in a perfect perm, and stood not quite five feet tall.

But from the moment we began talking, I knew she was one of those women who used her diminutive frame to her advantage. After introductions, we sat down, and she said, "Paisley Sutton, you have a knack for finding dead people. I admire that."

I stared at her a moment, trying to get a read on her tone, and then I stammered out, "Thank you, I think."

"You're most welcome. Amelia Peabody is a personal hero of mine, and you and she share some remarkable similarities. Are you familiar with her work?"

I laughed. "You mean as a detective or an Egyptologist?"

Mrs. Weatherby's smile grew wide. "In this instance, I was thinking as a detective, but I'm pleased to see you recognize her former talents as well." She took a demure sip of her drink. "And please don't think me rude for asking you not to involve your very handsome boyfriend. My concern is not that the police not know what I have to say but that, rather, what I have to say will be a waste of their valuable time."

I nodded. "I have found it's best to let Sheriff Shifflett decide for himself what is or is not a waste of his time. I'm sure you understand." Something about this woman made me want to speak as if I had just walked off the set of *Downton Abbey*, and I found that I rather liked my tone and syntax in this form.

"I do, my dear. Your boyfriend is quite competent at his job, and while I have not seen hide nor hair of chauvinism in him, we do live in a patriarchy, don't we?" She sighed. "It's best that we keep the menfolk a little clueless until we are ready for the complete overthrow of the system, don't you think?"

I looked down at the "Overthrow the patriarchy" pin on my jacket and grinned. "I actually think Santiago might like to be a part of that coup, but I do see your point."

She smiled. "Excellent. Now, to the body in the cabin. I can't give you anything specific about how it got there, but I can tell you that on the day you were set to demolish that fine building,

I was taking my daily constitutional along the Parkway. I enjoy the scenery and the fresh air, you see, and I was just passing the Sandy Bottom overlook when I noticed a young woman being, well it seemed to me, pushed into the back of a blue SUV." She let out a long breath. "I wasn't positive about what I had seen, but I did make a note of the license plate just in case."

She slid a pink post-it with the words "Smash the Patriarchy" across the top of it over to me. On it was a license plate number. "The plates were those Save the National Parks ones, if that helps."

I stared at her and then down at the paper. "This is a remarkable help, Mrs. Weatherby. Thank you." I tucked the paper into my wallet and smiled. "I will let Santiago know that you were a big help." I stood to go but then paused. "If I may, for someone as savvy as you are about misogyny and oppression of women, why do you introduce yourself by your husband's name instead of your own?"

"Subterfuge, sister. We have to keep them guessing!" Then she stood up and leaned over to my ear. "You can call me Nellie. We'll go by first names at the uprising."

I smiled and shook her hand. "Nice to meet you, Mrs. Weatherby," I said with a wink. "Thank you again."

Since I was just up the street from the station, I decided to walk over to share Mrs. Weatherby's information with Santiago. I could have texted him, of course, but given how abruptly our morning had started and the immense stress I knew he was under, I thought he might appreciate a re-creation of my conversation with our informant.

When I walked in, the station was in a frenzy with Savannah at her desk and Santiago talking to a couple of deputies in Orange County uniforms, and the phones were ringing off the hook. I wasn't sure exactly what was happening, but clearly both Santi and Savannah were far too busy for me to give them my update. I snagged a notepad from Santi's desk and jotted down the information Ms. Weatherby had just provided and handed him the sheet of paper, waited for him to look at it, and then give me a wide-eyed nod before I walked back out. The last thing they needed was me hanging around distracting them, and with the license plate number for the possible kidnapping vehicle on hand, they had everything I could help with.

The morning was already quite warm, so while I liked the idea of sitting outside and doing a little research, I opted to walk to Mika's shop to work instead. In contrast to the police station, the shop was remarkably quiet. I waved to Mika as I came in and headed to where she was working at the register. "Mind if I work here?" I asked with a smile and full awareness of her answer.

"Of course not. But this is a surprise. I thought you'd be over at the lot making sure Uncle Saul doesn't decide to decorate with power tools." She winked at me.

I feigned concern. "Is that a possibility?" I sighed. "Okay, I know it's a possibility, but given that we're having very expensive windows installed today, I think we may have a little time before he starts hanging up the nail guns as decor."

"Excellent. So tell me what brings you into town, then." Mika knew me well enough to understand that if I had the option to stay at home with my couch and my snacks and my cat, I would.

I caught her up on the information from Mrs. Weatherby and then filled her in on the adventure Saw and I had the night before. As expected, she was quite peeved that I had put the two of us at risk like I did, but when I explained that I had no way of knowing that people were camping illegally right where we were going to look, she calmed down a bit, even as she reminded me that it was good to let someone know where I was going most anytime, not just in the middle of a murder investigation.

I conceded the fact and then told her that I was going to try to get a head start on my newsletter and maybe finalize some sales, if she didn't mind me using her Wi-Fi.

"No problem at all. But sit in the front window, if you will. Makes me look busy." She winked at me and went back to her bookkeeping.

I plopped down in the upholstered chair by the window and got out my laptop. The crystal knob lady was thrilled with the price and asked if she could pick up her order on Friday. I agreed and then realized this meant I was going to have to figure out where I had my goods packed in my shed. Maybe Santi could drive me over there on lunch so I could do that this afternoon and also keep Saul from decorating on his own if the windows were, by some miracle, already done.

The rest of my email was pretty routine, a few quick responses to online auction queries, and I was clear to research and write. I'd had an idea to do a write-up on the families of Octonia who had been displaced by the park, but given the tensions lately, I decided to go another route and talk about ways to decorate with salvaged goods. I figured it would be a good thought exercise for the office and sales space, but I wondered if it might also prompt some sales, especially if I included a few eye-catching photos with key links to my options for sale.

Two hours later, I looked up and realized it was after noon and I was starving. I texted Santiago to see if he had time to grab lunch and run me to the lot, and his reply was almost immediate. *Yes, I need a break. Where are you?*

I let him know I'd meet him out front of Mika's store, and in five minutes, he pulled up in his regular sedan, which I took to be a sure sign he wanted to be off the clock for a bit. When I climbed in, he said, "I need a maple bacon bagel," and took off toward the bagel place east of town. I didn't point out that this was a bit out of the way for us to go to Saul's lot south of here because when this man expressed a need for a particular food, it was desperate.

We decided to eat on the porch overlooking the lake out back, and with our maple cream cheese and slabs of bacon on cinnamon raisin bagels, we were both in hog heaven. The pig jokes were flying for our entire meal, and it was clear neither of us really wanted to talk about the pressing issues before us. And they could wait for an hour while we decompressed.

Soon enough, though, Santiago moved our conversation to more serious matters, and he thanked me for getting him the license plate number. "It belongs to a man named Michael Collins. He's from Harrisonburg but has apparently worked in Octonia a few times over the years, mostly in warehouses."

"Do you have a picture?" I asked, both hopeful and hoping against hope that it wasn't the guy in the woods.

Santi turned his phone to face me, and I was looking at the large man who had chased my son and me up the hill. "That's the guy from the campsite," I said quietly.

"Glad to have your confirmation. We ran prints from the campsite, and his came up. But of course, it's good to know the man you saw was the driver." He put his head in his hands. "So this is good news, of course, but the bad news is that we lost him."

I felt the guilt from last night swell up in my chest again. "So then Katherine was probably there yesterday?"

Santi put his hand over mine. "We found a chain tied to a tree near the site, and we expect she was kept there."

"But how? She started a fire." I was trying to imagine a fire near a tree, but it wasn't aligning with the careful campsite I saw yesterday.

"She wasn't tied to the tree, exactly. But more like on a leash." He looked at me. "I have a theory. Want to hear it?"

There was a tenderness in his voice that made me think he was very eager to share his theory with me. "Sure."

"I think Katherine heard you and Sawyer and set the fire so you could find them." He studied my face. "You probably gave her hope, Pais." He squeezed my fingers.

I so appreciated his considerate theory, and I did hope he was right, that we had given her a little lift in some dark days. But we still hadn't rescued her, and we had been so close.

"Paisley, I know what you're thinking. You could not have rescued her. The cuff around her ankle was bolted with a combination lock. Even if you'd known it was her and gotten to her before Collins came back, you wouldn't have been able to free her." He put his other hand over mine. "There was nothing you could do."

I knew he was right. I knew that I had made the right choice to keep my son safe, but I still felt horrible. To be that close...I shook myself out of my self-pity and said, "I hear you. Do you think she dropped the ring on purpose?"

He nodded. "It seems likely, given how she left a trail from the campsite. I expect when she realized they weren't actually putting her in the vehicle, she kept the trail going."

"The battery?"

"Hard to tell. Could have been hers or just trash? Her prints aren't in the system, so it's hard to know." He sighed. "Tell me more about the UTV?"

I wished I knew more to tell him than that it was bright blue with lots of lights all around the front. "The tires were big, like it was made for mud." I only knew this because Sawyer loves to watch mudding videos. But remembering that made me think of something else. "Actually, Sawyer might know what kind it was. I can ask."

"Worth a try," Santi said.

"So what now?" I asked as I sipped the last of my coffee. I knew I could research Michael Collins if I got a bit more information from Santi, but I also knew that he wouldn't want me to do that.

"Well, when you came in this morning, it was a madhouse, as I'm sure you saw. That's because we put out the word that we were looking for Collins and the woman you saw, Barbara Keller." He showed me an image of the woman on his phone, and it was definitely the redhead we'd seen yesterday. "Apparently, they've been pretty out and about on the other side of the Blue Ridge, and the folks over that way had seen them in various shops and such."

"Confident, huh?" I paused. "Had anyone seen Katherine?"

"Not so far. My guess is that they didn't bring her down off the mountain. I expect the Durango in the overlook was a ruse to draw people into believing they'd gone a lot further away."

"It worked," I said. "These guys been in trouble before?"

Santi shrugged. "Little stuff. Some shoplifting. Petty theft. Nothing on this scale, though."

I sighed. "Any sign of them today?"

"Nothing yet, but we're hoping. The sheriff's office over there is going door to door at the small businesses near there, and they're putting out the word on the local news. We hope someone will have seen one of the three of them." I heard what Santiago was saying, but I didn't hear much hope in his voice.

"Any idea why they took her?" I asked.

"Nothing yet. But I'm hoping you can help with that. Can you see if there are ties between either of the kidnappers and the Fletchers or the O'Malleys?"

"Historically, you mean?"

"Yeah, I'm trying to figure out if this is something personal for Collins and Keller, or if maybe someone brought them in." Santiago sighed.

"Like kidnappers for hire?" Suddenly, this felt like something from a *Castle* episode.

"Or killers," he said with a shake of his head. "I feel way out of my league."

It was my turn to comfort him. "You know how to handle

this. You're great at your job, and while this isn't normal Octonia crime, just do what you always do. Follow the evidence one step at a time."

He gave me a small smile. "Thanks, Pais." He cleared our dishes. "Anything you can find that might rule out or rule in more information..."

"I'm on it," I said as I followed him to the door. "I'll get to work right away."

Unfortunately, "right away" wasn't quite as soon as I hoped it would be because when Santi dropped me off at Saul's construction lot, not only were all the new windows in but the floor guys were there to begin resurfacing the original wood Saul's crew had somehow managed to lay down while the window installers were there. When I walked in, Saul and two of his crew members were standing, hands on hips, staring at the floor as if they thought maybe it would tell them what to do next.

Two men with orbital sanders were standing on the other side of the room studying the three construction guys, and I was so tired and overwhelmed by everything that I started to giggle at what could have been the first Wild West standoff over flooring in history. Fortunately, the angry glances all five men shot my way pulled me back to reality, and I quickly instructed the sanders to simply take off the existing finish because the boards were thin and wouldn't withstand a deep sanding.

Then, while they got to work, I asked Saul and his crew members to walk with me to the shed, where I pulled out two corbels to use as choices for our floor stain. One was finished in a deep mahogany with a little sheen, and the other was bare oak that had grayed over the years. The surface was slightly rough and completely matte. We quickly agreed the gray oak was too close to the color of the logs and opted for the mahogany but with a matte finish.

As I had help in the shed, I enlisted the men to help me

locate the three totes full of crystal doorknobs, and when we'd located them, one of the guys brought a Gator around to carry them to the house, where the buyer was planning on picking them up in two days. I was pleased to move the merchandise especially since I knew that new projects would bring in even more of those knobs. I wasn't going to be without that stock for long.

Back in the house, I relayed the color choice to the floor crew, and then I settled into my future office to begin the research that Santiago had requested I do. Very quickly, I ruled out Michael Collins as having any ties to the area around the park. His family had moved down from New Jersey just two generations ago, and before that, they had been in the US for generations. I couldn't find anything that tied them to the O'Malleys, the Fletchers, or any of the other families that had settled around the park.

Barbara Keller's family, however, was another story. The Kellers had been residents of Octonia. Their property, while not quite adjacent to that of the O'Malleys and Fletchers, was close by. It was likely the families had known each other back in the day. I relayed that information to Santi right away, even though I had nothing definitive to tie the families together beyond land ownership.

He acknowledged the information and thanked me, but I knew that such a tenuous tie wasn't enough. I kept digging. I traced the Fletchers, O'Malleys, and Kellers all the way back to their emigrations from Ireland, and when I did that, I found something interesting. All the families had come over on the same boat, the *O'Shea*, which made me inclined to think they'd all known each other in Ireland. Without digging into Irish history, which would require a new genealogy subscription or a lot of overseas phone calls, I couldn't confirm that. But I figured close quarters on a transatlantic trip might be enough to prove the families at least had passing familiarity with each other.

I wanted to pin down more, though, so I went broader, using the matching generations of each family, and it was there that things got interesting. Apparently, the Keller family was known for their tanning operations up on the mountain. A few years after they established their farm, according to local papers, they opened a small market as well as their tanning business. Within a couple of years, they had a reputation as swindlers who overcharged for their goods and services but who had, by dropping trees on the road, essentially forced everyone on the mountain to shop with them. "The Mountainside Mafia," one neighbor called them.

I restrained myself from doing a search to find out when the word *mafia* came into use and kept my focus on the task at hand. As I moved forward in time, the Keller family shifted from controlling people by force into controlling them with goods. During Prohibition, they became the county's biggest moonshiners, and by the time the 1940s and '50s came around, they had a reputation as being the fixers for everything from local athletics to major elections in the area. Basically, they were the crime lords of Octonia.

But then, by the 1970s, when Santiago and I were growing up here, the family had gone largely quiet, at least as far as I could tell from public records and newspaper accounts. That fact answered a question I'd had about why I hadn't thought anything of Barbara Keller's name when it came up, and it also explained why Santiago hadn't recognized the name, either.

That said, I'd now been around enough police investigations to know that just because you don't see the actions doesn't mean they aren't there. I didn't have the resources to do the kind of digging required to see if – and how – the Kellers were still involved in nefarious pursuits, but I knew the person who did. I called Santiago and gave him the run-down.

"Glory be, Pais. You've uncovered the secret mob of Octonia." He laughed and then got very quiet on the other end of the line. "Can I ask you to do one more thing?"

I took a deep breath and said, "Sure. What would that be?"

"Write your newsletter about the Kellers...and send it out early." I could hear him breathing as he waited for my response.

"Let me get this straight. You actually want me to intentionally put my foot all the way into an active murder investigation?"

"I do," he said.

"And that investigation has clearly revealed ties to the family you just called the 'Octonia Mob'?"

"Right."

I took a deep breath and gave a little woot of joy. "You got it. Want to read it before I send it?"

"I do not," he said. "Plausible deniability. You'll get it right, and then we'll take it from there."

"I'm on it," I said with a quick glance at the time. I had an hour before I needed to be at Sawyer's school to pick him up, and I was going to make the most of that time. "Stay tuned."

Santiago laughed and then hung up the phone. I didn't even think. I just began writing.

Forty-five minutes later, I had told the story of the Kellers from their arrival in the US through the early years on the mountain and up until the story got quiet about 50 years ago. The pièce de résistance of the article was my final paragraph:

I HOPE the Keller family has forsaken their family's long tradition of subterfuge and crime. I really do. But if they haven't and you know what they're doing now, well, do tell.

. . .

I EXPECTED the gossipmongers of Octonia to be typing faster than the speed of light as soon as they opened this particular missive. So I loaded it up into my email service provider, scheduled it to send in ten minutes, and closed the computer. Now, I needed to go get my son and get him home before the rumors started flying and the Octonia Mob started coming after my family.

Fortunately, Santiago had considered a similar possibility and asked my dad and Lucille to meet us at home to keep us company. He hadn't told them why we needed company, but given my history with murder investigations, they didn't need to be rocket scientists to figure it out. Dad came in and said, "Okay, so who are we on the lookout for now?"

I smiled and sank into the couch while Lucille gracefully steered Sawyer outside to his playground. "The Kellers."

Dad sat bolt upright in the rocker across the room. "You're kidding, right? They aren't who Santiago is investigating. Right?"

I stared at him as I felt all the blood leave my face.

"For God's sake, Paisley, how are you involved with this investigation?" He looked angry enough to break the arms right off the rocker.

"I wrote an article about their family's history of crime and sent it out to my newsletter list today," I said very quietly.

Dad leaned forward, putting his good ear in my direction. "Did I just hear you say that you wrote about their family and sent it out in an email?"

I nodded. I had an instinct to throw Santiago under the bus for this one, but I was a grown woman. I made my own choices. "Tell me why that was a terrible idea?"

Dad slumped back. "I will, but first, we need to get some folks over here to help keep a presence. Saul and his crew at the lot?"

I nodded. Saul had taken me to pick up Sawyer again and

then run us home, but he'd gone back to supervise the guys on the floor since they were trying to finish up today.

"Good," Dad said as he took out his flip phone and dialed Saul's number. "Saul, you and your boys get to Paisley's right now. She wrote about the Kellers."

Apparently nothing further needed to be said because Dad hung up and looked at me. "The Kellers deal in black market organs."

For a moment, I got an image of people selling church organs out of the back of panel vans, but then I realized these were not the organs that Dad was speaking of. "Like kidneys?" I whispered.

Dad nodded. "It's an open secret around these parts. They can get you what you need if you need it...and if you have enough money to pay."

I shuddered. "All these people on the transplant lists, and these folks are trading in human parts. That's horrible."

"Horrible but lucrative, Paisley." He shook his head. "You've really stepped in it this time."

I sighed. He was right, and now, Sawyer was in danger yet again because of me. I took a deep breath and started to let my mind work through how I was going to keep us safe. Santiago would stay the night, so that would be good—

I didn't get any further with that line of thought because I suddenly realized that Santiago had no idea what he was stepping into. If he had, he would never have suggested I write that story. I jammed my finger into the screen of my phone by his picture and prayed he'd pick up.

Fortunately, he answered on the first ring. "I think we made a mistake, Pais."

"I think so, too," I said. "Why do *you* say that?"

"Because Lloyd Keller just walked into the station and demanded I arrest you for libel."

10

W ithin minutes, Santiago was at my house, and I saw a cruiser from Orange County sitting at the end of my driveway. In a brief flash of levity, I thought of installing a coffee bar there since I seemed to need police protection a lot. Coffee was the least I could do. Maybe I'd invest in a thermal carafe I could hand deliver on demand.

The wisp of humor died away when Saul and four of his guys showed up just moments later. Two of them took up posts on each of my two porches with Saul setting up shop by the back door. They didn't have rifles propped across their laps, but that was the only thing missing from making my house the second vision of the Wild West I'd seen that day. If this weren't all so serious, I'd probably have made a TikTok video about it all.

But it was serious, and when I sat down to talk with Dad and Santiago about the situation, it became very clear that Santi and I had made a grave error here. "Tell me about the Kellers," Santi asked my dad.

Dad shook his head. "They're bad news in the biggest way. I went to school with Lloyd and his sister Renee. They put on a great front – quarterback, homecoming queen, debate team, that sort of thing. But they were bullies through and through, and everyone from Octonia knew it."

Santi sat back and took a deep breath. "Tell me about their business?"

"They buy and sell human organs," Dad said.

A flush of red passed up Santi's face at Dad's direct statement. "Forgive me for asking, but how do you know?"

Dad looked up at the ceiling for a minute as he said, "That's a good question. It seems like I've always known. Let me think."

Santiago did not look relieved to find this to be the sort of knowledge that people just had rather than acquired, but he waited while Dad gathered his thoughts.

"It might have been something from church, I think. A few years back, one of our members got really sick, and they quickly discovered he had needed a heart transplant. He was older, nearing seventy, and it wasn't likely he'd be high on the list." Dad sighed. "It didn't look good, and while we all hoped and prayed for a miracle, the family also started preparing for his final days."

I wanted to ask my dad who this person was since his church was the church I'd grown up in and, in all likelihood, I'd know the person. But I knew my dad, and if he hadn't said the person's name to begin with, he wasn't going to share it.

"But then one day, at a potluck dinner, a friend mentioned that this man had gotten a heart. It was such a surprise, and I was happy to hear the news. But quickly, it became clear that there wasn't going to be a big celebration or even an announcement in the service. He just went from being on the prayer list to not." Dad shook his head. "Then he and his wife moved without ever coming back to church."

I sat forward. "So you think that he bought a heart?"

"I have no proof, but soon after, rumors started circulating about Lloyd's business, that it was just a front for organ trading. I put two and two together." Dad ran a hand down his face.

"What is Lloyd's supposed business?" I asked.

"Imports and exports," Santi said.

I actually laughed out loud. "Like in the movies? He couldn't have been more original?"

Santi gave me a small smile. "It's a hard business to track in terms of taxes and records. There's a reason it's the frequent cover in the movies."

I nodded and looked at Dad. "Have you heard of more instances?"

"Once I started paying attention, it became clear that a strange number of people were getting transplants in the area." He shook his head. "But what really told me that the rumors were true was when our neighbor suddenly came into enough cash to remodel his entire house."

"A lot of people renovate their houses, Dad," I said, trying to play devil's advocate although I knew my dad didn't jump to conclusions without careful thought.

"From a 1,600-square-foot rancher to a 7,000-square-foot mansion with a four-car garage, a new Porsche, and a fully landscaped English formal garden?" He raised his eyebrows as he looked at me.

"Whoa," I said under my breath.

"Right. And did I mention he was an eighth grade science teacher?" Dad said as he looked from me to Santi.

"Did you talk to him about it?" Santi asked.

"I did. We've been friends a long time, and I was happy for him. But I was worried that someone close to him had died and left him money. I didn't want him to be alone in his grief." Dad groaned. "But when I went to talk to him and see how he was, he said he was great and showed me a long scar below his rib cage."

"From surgery?" I asked, already knowing the answer.

"Liver surgery," he said. "I got to help someone and myself at the same time. Thank God for Lloyd Keller,' he told me."

Santi sat forward again. "He sold part of his liver to Lloyd?"

"I didn't ask for specifics because I didn't want to know more, but that's what I took it to mean." Dad drummed his fingers on his knee. "I've since heard similar stories about people who received and people who gave. I stopped asking questions, though, because when I did mention my suspicions to friends, everyone hushed me up quickly with warnings about not putting my nose where it didn't belong."

I looked over at Santi, and his face was as red as a radish now. I knew that look. He was furious. I reached over and put my hand on his knee. "I'm sure they worked really hard to keep things quiet."

Dad nodded vigorously. "I wouldn't even be telling you now if Paisley hadn't put herself right in Lloyd's crosshairs. It's wrong, what they're doing, no doubt, but the people who are participating know what they're getting into."

"Dad, you know that's just a rationalization, right? You should have told Santi," I said, feeling more than a little frustrated with my dad.

"No, Paisley, he's right," Santi said as he took my hand. "It's my job to know what's going on here, and I wouldn't want anyone to put themselves in danger." He squeezed my fingers and then looked at Dad. "Thank you for telling me now."

I wanted to scream at both of them, but now wasn't the time. I took a deep breath. "So what does all this have to do with Katherine Forester and Paul Fletcher?" I asked.

Dad sighed. "I have no idea, but I do know there is a connection. And now" – he turned to Santi – "you have to find it."

"I will, sir," he said. "It's my job, but I also care about your daughter very much. I won't let anything happen to her."

"I'm glad to hear that, son," Dad said and stood up. "I'm going out with Saul now. I need some fresh air."

For a few minutes after Dad left, Santiago and I just sat in silence holding hands. I don't know what he was thinking, but if it was anything like what I was thinking it included several swear words and a whole lot of variations on *what have we done*?

Eventually, I couldn't stew in my own miasma of regret any longer, and I went to see what Sawyer and his grandmother were doing. No surprise, they were playing down by the stream by the house, and apparently, Saw's Baba had a pretty good arm. As I walked up, she beaned a thin branch on top of a log across the stream because Sawyer asked her to. I was impressed since he had demanded the same of me, to no avail.

I spent a few minutes trying to redeem my reputation for having some athletic prowess and failing miserably, and only when I sat down to watch Sawyer try to splash his grandmother did I notice that Beauregard had followed me down. He'd taken up a perch on the top of the second bank above where we played, and he looked like the lord of the castle, a posture I'm sure he affected with completely conscious choice.

As I rested my head against the base of the large sycamore to soak in a little of the sun and give myself permission to be afraid and regretful and courageous all at the same time, I heard a strange sound rising up behind me. At first I thought it was the train coming around the bend a couple miles away, but the noise never got louder. It didn't have the sense of distance of an airplane engine, and vehicle traffic was a much more fleeting sound.

I sat up and looked around. When I pinpointed the source of the noise, I realized it was Beau, and he was growling. I stood up and followed his gaze across the stream into the treeline below my neighbor's house. There, in the shadows, I could just make out a figure watching us.

Without a second's thought, I swooped down and grabbed Sawyer under the arms and dragged him up the hill while also extending back a hand to help Lucille follow suit. Then, I shouted, "Run!" and forced Sawyer ahead of me and up the hill to the house.

To his credit, the boy didn't stop until he saw Santiago on the porch, and then he said, "Run, Santi. Someone's chasing us."

I caught the wash of confusion on Santiago's face as his eyes shifted to me. "In the woods across the stream. Just now." I was panting and couldn't get more out of my lungs

Fortunately, I didn't have to, because not only did Santiago hear me, but so did all the men guarding the house. As if they'd choreographed the action, Saul, one of his crew, and Santiago sprinted toward the stream, and Dad and the other man stood up and blocked the doors.

As Santi ran, I saw him take out his radio and shout something into it. A moment later, the cruiser from the end of the driveway was at the house, and the officer was out of it and ushering Lucille, Sawyer, and me inside the house as he called for backup. Then he closed all the blinds and told us to sit together on the couch. His demeanor was brusque and cold, and I was just about to remind him that a small child was present.

But then he picked up the remote, looked at Sawyer, and said, "*Frozen* or *Frozen Two*?"

"The one with the horse pushing Elsa under water," Sawyer said with all seriousness.

The officer didn't bat an eye and said, "*Frozen Two* it is" and navigated straight to the movie before handing me the remote and saying, "I have three of my own," before smiling at me. "You take care of him, and I'll take care of you," he said as he walked into the kitchen to take up his post at that door.

I stared after him for a minute, but then I did as I was told.

And while I watched *Frozen Two* with my son for the sixth or seventh time, I found myself torn between being grateful that things are not always what they seem and being terrified of exactly the same thing.

At least two other patrol cars arrived while Elsa and Anna tried to figure out what was calling them into the mountains, but I let the deputy on the scene take care of things. He had been right. My job was to take care of Sawyer, and between Lucille and me, we were actually able to respond to his many requests to "watch this" and still rest a little.

About a half-hour after we'd done our hundred-yard-dash from the stream, Santi, Saul, and the deputy came back into the living room. Santi motioned toward the front porch, and Lucille and I followed him outside while Saul took up the post on the couch with Sawyer. When I heard him say, "So who is Elsa going to freeze this time?" I felt confident he had the situation well in hand.

On the porch, Santiago said they hadn't found anyone there, but he did see footprints and had followed them back to the road above my neighbor's house. "Definitely a man. A big man, I'd guess. We'll get measurements and prints. See if we can't narrow it down."

I looked at him closely, and he gave his head a little shake. So I kept my mouth shut. I'd ask my question later.

Dad wanted to know what Santi was going to do to keep Sawyer and me safe. "I'm staying here tonight," Santi began, "and if you two are willing" – he looked at the deputy who had been up at the road and the one who was an Elsa and Anna fan – "I'll ask you to stay on site, too."

Both men nodded without hesitation.

"Good," Santi said. "Now, who wants dinner on me?"

No one actually raised a hand, but there was a sort of collective agreement that settled into the air. Santi picked up the phone and ordered a wide array of Mexican food to be delivered. I was grateful because, to be honest, I hadn't thought at all about feeding even Sawyer and me, much less all these helpful and hungry people.

A short time later the food arrived, and Savannah pulled up just about the same time. She'd gotten a few hours of sleep and was coming to help guard us overnight. It was quickly decided that the deputies would split the night so that each of them could catch a few hours on the couch. Savannah agreed to sleep in Sawyer's bed if, and only if, she could have the pleasure of Beauregard's company. I didn't have the heart to tell her that "pleasure" wasn't exactly the word I'd use to describe what it was like to sleep with a huge, grumpy cat who used his claws freely if you crossed what he deemed to be his territory, which was about two-thirds of the bed. But she seemed excited by the prospect of cat fur in her face at night, so I didn't argue.

Dinner was casual and a bit stiff, since everyone's guard was fully up, but everyone ate well and talked a little. It wasn't the ideal entertaining-dinner-table conversation, yet I was glad to share a meal with these fine people.

After we ate, Saul and Dad reviewed the plans for guarding us all with Santi and the deputies, and the trained police officers reassured these two older men that everything was going to be fine.

"Good," Saul said. "Now, I'm off to sleep at Mika's place. Can't be too careful."

Santi nodded. "I like that plan." He turned to Dad and Lucille. "Do you want me to send an officer out your way?"

My dad kept himself from rolling his eyes, but I could feel the vibe nonetheless. "That won't be necessary, Santiago," he said. "I've got Lucille here to protect me."

"Darn right," she said, and the two of them headed off to their car.

As soon as they were out of earshot, Santi said, "I'll have a patrol go by every hour or so."

I took a deep breath. "Thanks." I hadn't really let myself think about who else might be in danger because of the letter, but now that I was, Mika and my parents were high on the list. "I think I should let Mary know what's going on, too."

Mary Johnson had quickly become one of my dearest friends, and while she had even fewer ties to this case than Mika, whose shop was one of my commonly known work spaces, I still wanted to give her a heads-up.

"Good idea. Maybe she can stay with friends for a few days?" Santi suggested.

While he and Sawyer managed the dishes with far more soap than was necessary, I stepped back onto the porch to call Mary. As soon as she answered, I told her about the situation, suggested she maybe stay somewhere else for a few days, and then said, "Also, could you ask some folks to pray?"

"Of course, Paisley. I'll do it discreetly, but of course. And if it will make you and Santi feel better, I'll go into Richmond and stay with my sister for the rest of the week. Be good to see her anyway."

"That would make me feel better. Thank you. I'll keep you posted."

"You better," she said before hanging up.

With all the adults I loved cared for, I most needed to take care of the little human in my house. Fortunately, even with all the hullabaloo, Saw was right on schedule with his routine: at a little after six, even Beauregard's presence in the same room drove my son to rage, and so I knew he was at his normal place for the night.

I shooed everyone to the porch, gave Sawyer his nightly videos and chocolate milk, and sat down beside him to try and meditate for a few minutes. When Saw shook me awake a bit later and said he was ready to go to bed, I made an executive decision to do the same. I let Santiago know I was headed up for the night, and then I got Sawyer into pjs, into the bathroom, and into bed in short order. Within minutes, he was asleep, and I was trailing close behind.

THE NIGHT WAS UNEVENTFUL, if you count one of the best night's sleeps I'd had in months as *uneventful*. But since I didn't wake in the night with a murderous human organ trader standing over me ready to take out my lungs while I still needed them, I counted it as uneventful.

As I started to stir, I felt a tiny hand reach over and wiggle under my chin. I wasn't really ticklish there, but I wasn't about to tell the cutest boy on the planet that, even if he did think tickling was an appropriate way to wake someone up.

I tickled him a bit, and then I whispered, "Where do you think Santi is ticklish?"

Sawyer got a gleam in his eye and rolled over to where Santi was still sleeping. Then, the boy jumped on the man and said, "Gotcha!" before shoving his little fingers into the man's armpit and wiggling for all he was worth.

Santiago held his own by feigning sleep for a good three minutes, but then I figured if we were up, he needed to be up, too, and went for his feet. Clearly the man had tender feet because he hefted that boy off himself and got his feet into his shoes before I even got warmed up. But then, he grabbed Saw under the arms, tossed him back in the bed, and tickled him breathless.

Sawyer was so happy when the three of us made our way downstairs. Savannah was already up, and God bless her, she'd already made coffee, too. "Hope you don't mind," she said as she poured me a cup.

"Mind?" I asked. "Can you move in?"

She smiled. "That bed was really comfortable, almost like new," she said with a wink and a glance in Sawyer's direction.

"I've heard that same review from other reputable sources," I replied. "Glad you slept well."

Santiago had stepped out onto the porch off the kitchen, and when he came back, the two slightly rumpled deputies joined him. "All's quiet," he said as he headed toward the fridge and took out two pounds of bacon and a dozen eggs that I didn't even know I had. When he saw my face, he said, "I ordered in."

Savannah took a bow. "I aim to please, especially if bacon is involved," she said.

As Santi and Sawyer cooked, I got the officers clean towels and directed them to make themselves at home. While everyone washed up and got their own mugs of Savannah's coffee, Sawyer recruited police officer after police officer for some epic games of tractor race and hide and seek. I loved seeing him so happy in his little extroverted self, and once again, I was thrilled he was going to school so he could get more of a social life than his introverted mama was going to give him.

With bacon, scrambled eggs, and buttered toast on the table, we all squeezed in to eat. I gave Sawyer my phone so he could watch videos, and while I reminded everyone to keep in mind that just because he didn't look like he was paying attention didn't mean he wasn't paying attention, I did say, "This has to all be connected, right? It's just not possible that all this stuff is coincidence."

"Definitely not coincidence," Savannah said. "We found Collins's car down in Elkton. It had been sitting in the Sheetz parking lot for five days. The manager had called to have it towed, but he agreed to leave it on site for the sake of our investigation."

"That's good," I said tentatively, not sure the relevance of this information since we already knew that the Durango belonged to Collins.

"Well, yesterday, the manager called me to ask if I'd decided to have the car towed after all because it was gone." She waggled her eyebrows at me. "I told him we had not, but I appreciate the heads-up."

"Then you activated the tracking device you'd placed under the bumper?" I said, getting all caught up in the story.

All four officers at the table laughed out loud, and I'm pretty sure one of the deputies chuckled so hard he got coffee up his nose.

"No," Savannah said with a smile and a patronizing pat on my hand. "I informed the sheriff's department, and they began a search for the car. They found it parked at a place up by Sherando Lake."

"Was Collins there?" I said.

"Not yet," she said, "but the place is under surveillance. If he or anyone else shows up, we'll know."

I sighed. It wasn't the kind of news I'd been hoping for, but at least it was something. "Let's hope more comes of that soon." I glanced over at the oven clock and realized that Sawyer was about to be late for school.

As I hustled him into clothes and got his lunch packed, Savannah offered to drop him off and let him work the siren for his friends when he got there, if he wanted.

And boy, did he ever want. He was bouncing up and down beside her cruiser for the entire time it took Santiago to switch the car seat over. I'm pretty sure he might have waved once at me as they pulled out.

The two other officers were going off shift, but they stayed a bit and had another cup of coffee while we waited for their replacements to take up the watch. The part of me who hated to be a burden to anyone wanted to protest, but the other part of me, the part that had been actively avoiding opening my email out of fear, was grateful someone else would be on site for the day.

Once the shift change had taken place and a new officer was installed in the driveway with a fresh mug of coffee, I told Santiago I was going to read my email. He poured me a full mug, added extra creamer, and sat down beside me. "I'm here. Let's do this," he said.

When we opened my inbox, I gasped. I had over ninety messages, at least forty of which were direct responses to my newsletter. Out of habit, I quickly ran through and deleted all the advertisements and promotions, but then, I still had a whopping number of messages to go through.

"Maybe get out a pen and paper?" I said.

"Good idea," Santiago said and grabbed some drawing paper and a purple marker from Saw's stash. "I'm ready."

I smiled at how cute he looked with that giant marker in his hand and then clicked on the oldest message, received just twenty minutes after the email went out. It read, *Be wise, woman. You're treading on dangerous ground.*

Santiago made a note of the signature – *Concerned Friend* – and the email address before I moved it to a new folder for "Keller Stuff" and clicked the next one. Of the forty-seven messages I received in response to my email newsletter, forty-two of them were warnings like this one from people who clearly knew the Kellers were dangerous, wanted me to know it too, but didn't feel safe or eager enough to share more information.

It was the five other messages that were what were actually useful though. The first came from someone who identified herself as "Cat Lover 89." She told me a story that sounded much like my dad's. A friend of hers had been on the transplant list for a pancreas. No one was very hopeful she'd get it, but then one day, out of the blue, she came over, asked the emailer to take care of her cat, and said she had to have an operation and couldn't come back to her house after that. Apparently, the house had stayed empty until it was foreclosed on, and if the woman hadn't brought by the cat, the sender and all her neighbors would have simply thought the woman died.

Three of the other messages were simple notes that said something like, *I have no proof, but they buy and sell kidneys and hearts and stuff on the black market.* No more details. Nothing identifying the writers except their emails.

But the fifth email was the one I won't ever forget. It was from Renee Keller, Lloyd Keller's sister and one of the bullies my dad had gone to school with. The email was a formal cease and desist letter from her as the legal representative of her family. In a long message that was so full of legalese that I had to read it three times to be sure I understood, she ordered me to stop writing about the Keller family and threatened to bring me up on formal as well as civil charges if I did not stop pursuing this line of inquiry in "every form." The letter was sent from her law office's address, and so I guessed that if I continued to ask public questions about things, I would, indeed, be sued and taken to court.

For some reason, the idea of someone taking an architectural salvager to court for libel struck me as quite funny, and the giggles came over me. Santiago looked at me carefully and said, "What are you imagining now?"

I looked at him, put on a straight face and lowered my voice to say, "Your Honor, thank you for allowing me to address you at the bench. Could you tell me if this is vintage oak or is it elm?"

Santiago rolled his eyes, but I saw him crack a smile. "You do know this is serious, right?"

"As if I didn't before, when the cavalry rolled out last night. But yes, I get that she's not bluffing." I sighed.

"Or maybe she is. But either way, we're not going to have you push any further into this at all." His voice was firm, and he held my gaze when he spoke.

"You do realize I need to follow up with the cat lady, right? I mean, she wrote to me." I knew I was pushing here, but I couldn't help myself. Once I got started on a story, I just couldn't quit it until I had as much information as there was to have.

"I will follow up with her, once I figure out who she is."

He sounded serious, and I knew I was treading on the thinnest of ice. "If you go see her, she'll know you read her email. These people thought they were writing to me in confidence. I need to go."

My boyfriend stared at me for a minute as if trying to figure out if I was cracking another joke or maybe running a high fever that made me delusional. But when I didn't flinch, he said, "Are you serious about that?"

"As serious as I am about liking dark coffee." This was, for me, the most serious of comparisons.

Santiago let out a long, slow sigh. "You are absolutely infuriating sometimes, you know that," he said.

"That's part of why you love me," I said as I got up and headed toward the stairs to get dressed.

"I might say I love you despite this particular character trait, but same difference." He followed me up the stairs, and we spent a little more time together before he went to the office and I went to visit the cat lady. I was fairly certain all was forgiven when we went our separate ways, me with yet another deputy following behind in an unmarked car.

11

T he Cat Lady of Octonia, as I began thinking of her while I drove to her house, lived in a little development called Grant over at the edge of the mountain range. The houses were lovely, mostly chalet style with good views of the mountains from every angle, it seemed.

Savannah had sent me the address via text before I even left my driveway. Her message read, *Be careful. Have my number ready to go. Get to the officer if you need help.*

I couldn't imagine a woman who took in her neighbor's cats and who had taken the time to share a story that might implicate the most notorious crime family of Octonia was someone I needed to fear, but I heeded Savannah's warning and called up the deputy's contact so I could just press send if I needed her.

As I pulled up in front of the address, the first thing I noticed was the lovely Japanese garden that graced the front of the house. Two stunning Japanese maples flanked a beautiful pond with a small waterfall running to it, and a small pagoda sat at one side with a perfect view of the pond and the mountains beyond. The place looked profoundly peaceful, and if I hadn't been there with a fairly morbid purpose, I might have suggested we sit in the pagoda to talk.

When I rang the bell, I heard a beautiful chime sound inside, and I waited to hear the sound of footsteps echoing across the floor toward me. A car was in the driveway, so I assumed that in all likelihood someone was home.

But after a few moments and a second ring, it appeared I was mistaken. Given that I often missed the people in my own driveway, I decided to peek around the back of the house to see if maybe the Cat Lady was gardening in the back.

What I saw there left me speechless – it was the most tastefully decorated cat yard I had ever seen. Beams and platforms stretched from tree to tree underneath a massive canopy of screen netting. Water bowls were placed strategically on the ground and up in the air, and a bevy of brightly colored toys were strewn over every surface in the yard.

No less than ten cats were lounging or grooming or playing in the space, and when I saw the sleeping porch with a clear view of the sun and at least four more cats snoozing away in sunbeams, I realized that if something happened to me, I would need to ask this woman to take in Beauregard. I could even see a feeder with a timing device in one corner of the porch so that the kitties could have food on their regular schedule. I kind of wanted to live there myself.

But while the place was a feline paradise, I didn't see any sign of humans in the yard. As I walked back around the side of the house, I took the liberty of glancing in each window I passed, just to get a look at the house. I loved peeks into other people's homes. I always felt like I was getting a little window into the stories of their lives.

I was just passing the small window closest to the front of the house that seemed to belong to a powder room or some such. I looked in quickly and was just about to move on when my brain registered what looked to be a human leg prone on the floor. I shoved my way through the immaculate azalea bushes and put my face right to the glass. Sure enough, there in the doorway, were the legs of a person, the unmoving legs of a person.

Without hesitation, I dialed Savannah and shouted to her through my pocket as I ran to the front door. "Something has happened to the Cat Lady. Come quickly and send an ambulance." I didn't disconnect the call as I pounded on the front door and then tried the handle. It was unlocked, which wasn't surprising in such a rural area, and I barged in and blundered my way through a formal living room to where I thought I'd seen her legs.

Sure enough, a slim older woman with silver, chin-length hair lay sprawled on the marble floor outside the bathroom. I knelt down near her head and hoped that I would see her looking up at me, but instead, her eyes were the still gaze of the dead, a gaze I'd come to know too well.

I dropped back onto my butt on the floor and then said, loudly enough for Savannah to hear, "She's dead."

THE FIRST PERSON TO arrive on the scene, of course, was the young deputy who had been my escort for the day. He was there in less than a minute of me calling Savannah, and when he came in and saw the scene, he immediately moved me away from the body and began to search the house. I waited on the very comfortable and deep couch in the living room and tried to calm my breathing. I had found a lot of dead people in the last year or two, but it never got easier or less shocking.

Savannah arrived a few minutes later, and when the deputy told her the house was clear, she asked me to explain how I'd found the woman, one Esther Glavender, dead. I told her about checking the backyard and about glancing in the windows. "Maybe this time we can be grateful I'm nosy," I said in a half-hearted attempt at humor.

"Maybe," Savannah said and gave me a small smile. "Did you see anyone else?"

I shook my head. "Just her cats. There are like fifteen of them out back." I groaned. "Someone is going to have to take care of them all now."

"We'll worry about that in a bit," Savannah said. "Why don't you wait for Santiago outside? He'll be here in a minute."

I nodded and went out to the front stoop and sat down. I had a lot of reasons to be glad I didn't live in a suburban community, but today, I was especially glad for the distance between houses because it meant there weren't a bunch of neighbors gawking or asking questions. I could just sit and let the mountains calm me.

A few moments later, Santiago pulled up and came jogging over. "You're okay?"

"I'm fine," I said, "I mean, considering."

He nodded and said, "I'll be right back," as he went inside the house.

I looked out at the pond in front of the house and decided that if there was a time when I needed to sit in a meditation garden it was now. I made my way to the pagoda and found, with a small boost of delight, a meditation stool that had the view I'd imagined when I pulled up. I took a seat and let my breath slow down. Then, I closed my eyes and focused, letting my thoughts float by without engaging.

The next thing I knew, Savannah was standing beside me and saying, "Paisley, are you ready to give me a statement?"

I opened my eyes and let myself take one more deep breath before I answered. The peace of meditation had done it's work, and I nodded up at Savannah. "Sure."

I told her about my arrival, about how I had looked in the backyard, and how I'd peeked in all the windows before seeing Ms. Glavender's leg on the floor. "Then I called you and ran inside."

"How did you get in?" she said.

"The front door wasn't locked," I answered.

A small crease appeared between Savannah's eyebrows. "You're sure of that?"

"Positive," I said. "I just opened the door and walked in. Didn't think anything of it. I almost never lock my doors during the day."

"But you also don't have an expensive alarm system and a safe room," Savannah said as she made a note.

"She has a safe room in there?" I pictured all the billionaires from movies that had safe rooms in which they got trapped as part of an elaborate blackmail scheme. "Who was this woman?"

"I'll let Santiago tell you," Savannah said. She stood up and then offered me a hand. I appreciated it, given that getting off the meditation stool was far harder than it had been to get down onto it.

Santiago met us on the walkway that went to the driveway, and when he didn't suggest I go back inside, I took that as a sign it was time for me to leave. I looked around to see if *my* deputy was back in his car, but the driver's seat was empty. I glanced at Santiago. "I can just hang around here, in my car, if you want to keep everyone working the scene."

"Nope, I'm following you to your house, and I'm staying with you. Savannah had the station covered, and we've got a few deputies on loan given the now high-profile nature of this case," he said.

"High-profile?" I asked.

"Esther Glavender is the widow of Horatio Glavender, a

wealthy shipping magnate who made his money on the Missis-
sippi decades ago. He and his wife wanted to retire somewhere
quiet, where they and the cats they rescued could just enjoy
nature." He looked at me. "I guess we've been successful at
keeping her presence quiet if even you don't know about it."

"I had no idea. Never heard of them. That's a good thing, in
her book, I guess, if she wanted to keep a lower profile. You said
she's a widow?" I looked back at the beautiful and expensive
but not at all ostentatious house.

"Two years ago. Alzheimer's. Mrs. Glavender decided to stay
since this was her dream house, and as she told me, she loved
her neighbors." He looked at the four other houses on the cul-
de-sac. "Still, she was cautious. Kept her alarm on, her doors
locked. She knew what her kind of wealth might lead people
to do."

"So that's why it's so odd she left her door unlocked. I see." I
looked back at the house again.

"The door was unlocked? Yeah, that's odd," Santiago said as
he scanned the neighbors' houses again. "That means she must
have let her killer in."

I sighed. "You don't have to tell me, but how long has she
been dead?"

"We have to wait for the coroner's official report, but I'd say
at least a couple of days." He cleared his throat. "No one
noticed."

I glanced around at the houses near us. "Not really that
unusual, though. If I didn't have Sawyer and you, I could go a
week or maybe two without seeing another human being."

"True, but I'll need to talk to the neighbors anyway. Maybe
someone saw something." He didn't sound particularly
hopeful.

"And maybe you can find out from them who gave her the
cat? Follow up with that person?" I knew Santiago had already

thought of that, but I had an ulterior motive for asking. "Maybe you could use a second pair of ears since Savannah and your other officers are occupied."

"I don't even have the energy to try to argue. Come on," he said as he pointed at the next house up the road. "But you don't talk, okay?"

I made the universal sign for zipping my mouth shut and followed him out to the road. I knew this was a somber occasion, but I couldn't help but be a little excited to delve further into the investigation.

No one was home at the first house, and at the second one, the woman who answered the door said she hadn't seen Esther in about a week but assumed maybe she was just away visiting her friends or her children. "She traveled quite often," the woman said.

Our third stop proved more fruitful. The middle-aged man who answered the door was wearing a headset. When he saw Santi's uniform and ID, he said, "Ron, I have to go. Emergency in the neighborhood. Call you later." Then, he pulled the headset from his head and said, "Is this about Esther?"

"What makes you say that?" Santi asked as we followed the man into his large open-floor living area.

"Well, I hadn't seen her in a bit, and I was actually going to head over there later today to check in." He pointed to the couch and sat down himself in a leather club chair. "But that, plus the fact that a strange car was sitting in front of my house for a few nights in a row and watching Esther's house made me nervous."

"How did you know he was watching Esther's house?" I asked and gained a quick glance of disapproval from my boyfriend.

"Oh, I asked him," the man said. "The second night he was here I just walked out and asked if I could help him with something. He apologized for worrying me and said he was part of Esther's security detail, that there'd been some recent suspicious activity and he was just here to keep an eye on things."

"That made you suspicious why?" Santiago asked.

"Well, first, Esther doesn't have a security detail. Sure, she could afford one, but part of the reason she and Horatio moved out here was so that they could avoid attention and scrutiny." The man sighed. "They were such delightful people."

"So you knew who they were?" Santi continued.

"I did. All of us here in the neighborhood did, actually. They were very up-front about themselves, said it took away the mystery if they just told us who they were from the get-go. I admired that about them."

I had to admit that seemed smart. Privacy is one thing, but secretiveness, especially in a place like Octonia, could really turn neighborly curiosity into a full-fledged investigative query by neighbors with Google.

"Did you let Mrs. Glavender know about the car?" Santi asked.

"I did, and she said she was aware. That she was staying in and had the alarm set." I should have gone over or called you guys, but that alarm system she has is top-notch. I thought she'd be safe."

"Could you describe this man to a sketch artist?" Santi asked.

"Absolutely. I'll come right down and do that if you'd like." He watched Santiago stand.

"That would be excellent. Thank you." Santiago shook the man's hand. "Oh, one more thing. What kind of car was this person in?"

"2017 Dodge Durango. Wrote down the plate if you want it." The guy headed toward a small table next to the windows at the back of the house. "Here you go."

"You've been most helpful. Thanks." Another handshake and we were headed toward the door.

I suddenly remembered the cats. "Do you know which of your neighbors gave Mrs. Glavender a cat recently?"

"Oh yes, that would have been Stuart. He lived in the house next door to the Glavenders. Broke his heart to give up Mitzy, but he just couldn't have her at the retirement home he was moving to in Florida."

"Do you have the name of where he went?" Santi asked.

The man stared into space for a few seconds, but then said, "I don't think he ever told me. I got the impression it was somewhere beachy, Miami maybe."

We thanked him again and walked back up the street, and by the time we were at the Glavender house again, the man had come out to his car and was headed, as promised, to the station. Santi had given them a heads-up that he was on his way, and they were expecting him. The sketch didn't seem that important now that we knew the person had been driving Michael Collins's car. But it was better to cover all the bases, I knew.

"Want me to find out more about Stuart?" I asked as I opened my car door.

"It's like you can read my mind," Santi said as he gave me a kiss on the cheek. "See you at your place. I'll be right behind you."

I smiled. I loved spending time with Santiago, but investigating a murder instead of enjoying a good movie and a nice dinner wasn't exactly ideal. Still, I knew it was an honor to be involved, so I didn't comment.

WHEN WE ARRIVED at my house, Santiago insisted I sit in my car with the doors locked while he did a search of the house and the land. After a few minutes, he came back and declared everything clear, and I got out of the car to find Beauregard sniffing around near the porch.

"Someone's been here," I said as I scanned the porch for packages that might have been brought by the delivery people.

Santi looked at me with a furrowed brow. "How do you know?"

I pointed to Beau, who was very intent on one patch of grass. "He knows."

"You can't be serious," Santi said.

"Oh yes, Beau knows," I said with a wink.

The groan from my boyfriend was exactly what I'd been hoping for with my throwback reference. "Seriously?" he asked.

"Actually, yes. He's not like a dog who can follow a trail, but he does know when someone has been here. He does this every time a package comes and we don't see the driver." I took another quick look at the porch. "But no packages today."

"I don't like this," Santiago said as he began another patrol of the outside of the house. "Let's get you and Sawyer some things and move you to my house."

I sighed. "I'm not even going to try and talk you out of this," I said in my best imitation of his voice. "Give me ten minutes."

If it had just been me, I would have thrown a change of clothes, some pajamas, and a few basic toiletries into a tote bag and called it done, but with a preschooler to accommodate, I had to get key toys, sleeping lovies, the right cups, select snacks, and the necessary clothes and toiletries for him too. Leaving the house for an afternoon with Sawyer could feel like I was packing for a weekend. Packing for a weekend felt like I was doing another semester abroad, but without weight limits on the luggage.

Still, I had lots of practice, and within my allotted time I had our five bags full and ready to go. We left my car in the driveway, securely locked, and we triple-checked the doors and windows of the house, leaving a light on upstairs just in case.

Santiago was going to send a car out this way at dusk anyway, but until then, it felt better to lock her up tight.

Beauregard, for once, was eager for an adventure and jumped into the back seat of Santiago's cruiser like he was entering his own personal limo. I didn't remind him that he was actually in the same spot that people under arrest rode. I didn't want to ruin his good mood.

At Santi's I set myself up at his dining room table with my notebook and laptop, and while he made me a fresh cappuccino from his machine, I got to work. It took me no time at all to locate Stuart Massie on the deed to the property at Grant. Then, it was just a matter of some savvy internet searches to discover he was, indeed, living in Miami, at a retirement village called Palm Winds.

I passed the information along to Santi, and while he made that phone call, I jotted down some notes about the case – or cases, as we had several now. I began by making a list of all the victims involved: Paul Fletcher, Katherine Forester, and now Esther Glavender. Then, I listed the suspects beginning with Michael Collins and Barbara Keller and adding in Lloyd Keller, Renee Keller, and even Patrick and Frank O'Malley.

Then, I started drawing lines to how people were connected to one another. Paul and Katherine had ties to the same area of land. Paul and the O'Malleys were connected by the land historically, as were the Kellers. Collins and Barbara Keller had kidnapped Katherine. All those connections were linked, very concretely, to the mountain land. But Esther Glavender was the odd woman out. She had a very loose feline tie to the Kellers through Stuart Massie and his alleged organ purchase, and Michael Collins had been staking out her house. But what I couldn't figure out was how the Kellers had known Esther had suspicions. I just couldn't put that piece together.

I stared at my notes for a long minute, but I knew that I wasn't going to magically pull the connecting thread up from the ink. I needed more information. Fortunately, from what I could hear on Santiago's side of the call, he was getting a lot further than I was.

While he talked and made a lot of notes, I decided to bake. Sometimes, I needed to be moving and distracted for my thoughts to come together fully, and besides I really wanted a snickerdoodle. I mixed the dry ingredients and then whipped the coconut oil shortening, sugar, eggs, and vanilla until smooth before I added the flour. All the while, my brain was turning things over, trying to figure out how the Kellers could have known what Mrs. Glavender knew.

As I rolled cookie dough balls in cinnamon and sugar and placed them on the trays, I let my mind wander to the cats in the back yard. I wondered which one had belonged to Stuart Massie, and then I decided to let my anxiety about where they would go now that their owner was dead rise to a fever pitch. It was easier to think about them, after all, than about Katherine Forester.

When Santiago finished his phone call, my hands were covered in dough and sugar, and I was near tears thinking about the fact that those poor cats might be euthanized. Santi took one look at my face and said, "Oh no. What's wrong?" He got up and came over to me by the stove.

The tears fell then. "The poor cats. What's going to happen to the cats?" I leaned, face into his chest, being sure to keep my hands up and away from his uniform. "Will they have to be put down? Maybe I could take them?"

Santi laughed into my hair. "First of all, you do not need sixteen cats. Second of all, Beauregard would kill them all."

As if on cue, Beau let out a small mew from where he'd made himself comfortable on Santiago's couch.

"But third, those cats are going to be fine. Mrs. Glavender had arrangements made for them in her will. Savannah found it, along with two full file drawers of veterinary records, in the study. The cats get to stay in the house, and Mrs. Glavender left means to hire a permanent caretaker to live in and be a companion for them. I expect her lawyer will put out an ad for the position right away." He pulled me back and looked at my face. "The cats are going to be fine."

I appreciated his comfort, but now I was more amazed than worried. "She had enough money to give her house to her cats?"

"Basically, yes." He studied my face and then took a cookie off the tray and popped it into his mouth raw.

"You're going to get salmonella," I said with a roll of my eyes.

"Then we'll die together," he said as he wiped a bit of cookie dough off the corner of my mouth. "Now, what's this really about?"

I slid the first tray of cookies into the oven. "Katherine," I said. "That poor girl."

"We're getting closer, Pais. We're going to find her." He pointed to the table. "Want to hear what Stuart Massie had to say?"

"Do you have to ask?" I said as I grabbed a cookie dough ball and followed him back to the table. "Sounds like he had a lot to say?"

"Oh yes, when he heard about Mrs. Glavender, he told me everything. He felt terrible."

"Terrible enough to admit he bought a body organ on the black market?" I said.

"Well, not that terrible. He didn't really give me that information, but he did say that he gave Mrs. Glavender Mitzy because he needed to leave town quietly and quickly. Apparently, he and Mrs. Glavender had talked cats quite a bit, so he knew she would care for his 'baby'" – Santiago made air quotes – "well. He gave her everything Mitzy owned and all her care records, and then he never looked back."

"Okay, well, that's good information, but it doesn't get us any further, does it?" I was feeling frustrated, and I could hear it in my voice.

Santiago grinned. "That information doesn't, no. But Stuart hinted very strongly that I might want to look closely at the papers he gave Mrs. Glavender. I have the feeling he may have left a little insurance policy for himself with his cat."

"Where are the papers now?" I asked, ready to jump out of my seat to start poring through them.

"Savannah will be here shortly with everything from the house. Feel like looking through documents, love?"

"Oh, you do know how to make a girl swoon," I said as I batted my eyelashes.

An hour later, the cookies were done, the house completely cleaned, and the yard weeded. I could not sit still, so I went to work doing things that didn't really need to be done because Santi kept his house very well and his yard even better. Still, the movement did help, and when Savannah arrived with four file boxes of papers, I was ready to sit down and sort through.

In addition to paperwork, Savannah also brought subs, so we sat on Santi's back deck and enjoyed a quick lunch before diving in. Between the turkey bacon ranch sandwich and the half-dozen snickerdoodles I had eaten, I was feeling quite content as we began to sort through the papers.

Unsurprisingly for someone who had built cat heaven in her backyard, Mrs. Glavender's records on her cats were neat and organized. It took only a minute or two for Santiago to locate Mitzy's file. As he flipped through the pages, he read off what each sheet was. Mostly they were vaccination and grooming records – Mitzy was apparently the white Persian I had seen lounging in the sun. Her coat was gorgeous and, as I knew from having a long-haired cat myself, did require a bit of extra care.

But as Santiago flipped to what I thought would surely be another record of a trim for Mitzy's mane, he stopped and stared. "Holy Mother of God," he said.

My head snapped up from where I had been staring at the immaculate records for fourteen other cats. That was Santiago's most extreme phrase, used only for situations when another person might have pulled out a major swear word. "What?!" I said, barely restraining myself from ripping the paper out of his hand to read it.

"Stuart Massie, you smart little devil," he said as he turned the papers around. "These are copies of all his emails with Lloyd Keller detailing the arrangements for his purchase, his surgery, and his agreement to leave town to avoid raising suspicions."

"Holy Mother of God is right," Savannah said as Santi handed her the papers. "This is everything we need to arrest Lloyd Walker for organ trafficking."

"Yes, yes it is," Santiago said.

"But Massie didn't want to admit anything?" I said, puzzled about why he'd point Santi to these records if he wouldn't actually tell him anything.

"Oh, I expect we'll find that Mr. Massie has moved on from his current residence if we try to contact him again." Santi said with a wry smile. "And truth be told, I'm not really inclined to hunt him down. We have enough to do as it is."

I nodded. This was one of the reasons I loved this man. He knew the law. He respected it, but he also didn't abide by this idea that every broken law was equal. I could get behind this plan of his. "All right, so now what?"

"Now, we make sure our ducks are in a row, and we make an arrest. Savannah, you good with calling the DA?" Santi asked.

"On it," she said and went out to the back porch with her phone in hand.

Santi and I checked through everything else that she'd brought while she finished her call and went to get the paperwork in order to arrest Lloyd Keller. Almost everything else in the files was truly pet care stuff, but I was sorting through the last file, marked "Personal Documents," when I came across the piece I had been missing earlier.

"Santiago, look at this," I said and handed him the sheet of paper.

He read it, stood up, and said, "We have to go. Now."

I didn't ask any questions. Just got up, put my phone in my pocket, and followed him back to his car. The papers I'd found were part of Mrs. Glavender's final wishes. She had been very specific about how she wanted her body used after she died. Her orders were that any viable organs be donated – "without intervention from anyone associated with the Keller family of Octonia, Virginia" – to those on the University of Virginia Transplant list.

It was that phrase about the Kellers that had made Santiago react.

She nodded and turned back around as we followed behind. "The artist just finished with Mrs. Glavender's neighbor. This guy look familiar, Paisley?"

I studied the charcoal drawing and saw the face of Michael Collins looking back at me. "Yep, that's the man who I saw at the Parkway overlook. The one who chased Sawyer and me." I knew better than to name him since, technically, I shouldn't know his name.

"Very good," she said and then turned to her boss. "We have a solid connection between the Kellers, Collins, and Glavender, then. Should be easy enough to get the warrants. I'm off to see the judge now." She turned and walked out the door toward the courthouse behind the police station.

I watched her walk for a minute, stunned by how all this was coming together, and when I turned around, I realized Santiago had disappeared. I looked around for a minute, and then I heard him say, "In here, Pals."

I followed the sound of his voice to his office and said, "You're like a magician."

He grinned. "I think you may be a little tired. Want to take a nap? I can wake you up when it's time to go get Sawyer."

I took a quick look at my phone. "Actually, that sounds nice, but I think I'd like to see Mika instead. Feel okay with me walking up there on my own?"

"Nope, but I'll escort you and then come pick you up later." He put out his arm, and I let him lead me out the back door and through the series of alleys that ran behind Main Street. I gathered he didn't think it wise for me to be parading down the center of town at the moment.

Once I was in through the back door of Mika's shop, he told me to stay in the back of the store, try to not be seen, and he'd pick me up in 90 minutes. I agreed, but after he left, I looked at Mika and started to laugh. "I may have just inadvertently entered witness protection," I said.

"Ooh, what's your new name? No, let me." She tapped a finger on the side of her head. "Myrtle Bagbalm. No, too farm-ish. They'll know you're from somewhere rural. Cooper St. Clair. No, too posh. Ooh, I know. Melody Orlando... Ooh, that's perfect. Nice to meet you, Melody."

I rolled my eyes and sat down in the Cozy Nook. "Are you done? Because I have big news."

"I'm done," she said and then stared at me, waiting.

I gave her the low-down on Esther Glavender and Stuart Massie and told her about the files and Mrs. Glavender's final wishes.

"Well, I'll be. Those suckers are going to be caught," Mika said as she slapped her leg.

"Seems so," I said. "And that's good."

"But?" Mika said with annoyance. "I hear that but."

"But it doesn't explain Paul Fletcher's murder or Katherine Forester's kidnapping. I mean, I'm glad Mrs. Glavender will get justice, but where is Katherine?" I could feel that knot of guilt beginning to expand again.

Mika sat back in her chair. "That's a good question."

"You're sure?" I said as I jumped up and started to run toward the front door to see if I could see someone walking away.

"Positive," Mika said as she snagged my arms. "You heard Santiago. Stay out of sight. I'll look."

I groaned and stopped. "Okay," I said as I walked back to the Nook and took out my phone to text Santi. *Someone heard me telling Mika. We may have a problem.*

Santi's text was short but clear. A swear word followed by *Be right there.*

Mika joined me again in the sewing circle and said, "I couldn't tell who it was. It's pretty busy out there. Sorry."

I shook my head. "I didn't even hear anyone come in."

"Me neither," she said as her forehead wrinkled. "That's weird. I mean, I guess they could have been in here awhile and I forgot."

I looked at my best friend. "No offense, but this place isn't exactly the Palace of Versailles."

This time, she rolled her eyes at me. "I know, but it's

amazing where people stay out of sight in here. I've been startled by a fair number of shoppers tucked into the nooks and crannies behind the yarn."

"So you think someone was hiding in here?" I said.

"Maybe. Or maybe I just lost track of them, they decided not to make a purchase, and left."

I sighed and let a tiny spark of hope stay alive with that prospect.

SANTIAGO WAS NOT happy when he picked me up, but Mika and I told him everything we knew, which was basically nothing, and explained what we'd been talking about.

"So this person overheard that we're about to arrest Lloyd Keller?" He let out a long hard breath through his nose. "I need to talk to Savannah."

"Maybe she's already arrested him?"

"We can hope," he said as he put the phone to his ear.

There was a lot of small hope floating around here at the moment.

Fortunately, a second later, a smile flashed across Santi's face as he listened to Savannah on the other end of the line. A moment later, he hung up and looked from me to Mika. "We got him."

WITHIN HOURS, not only Lloyd Keller but Renee and Barbara Keller, too, had been picked up and charged with trafficking human organs. After Lloyd's office was raided, the police found evidence implicating Renee and her daughter in the operation, and soon, everyone related to the crimes was in custody, including the doctors who had performed the surgeries. The business was officially shut down.

The Kellers and Michael Collins were all charged with organ trafficking, and Collins was charged with Esther Glavender's murder. None of them said anything once they were Mirandized, and their lawyer was some hotshot from Richmond. Santiago figured they'd post bond and mount a massive defense when the cases came to trial. But with the evidence he had, he was sure they'd be put away for a long, long time.

I was thrilled for him, but as I lay beside Sawyer that night, I was still bothered by Katherine Foster's kidnapping – Collins and Keller had refused to tell Santi or Savannah her location – and Paul Fletcher's murder. I knew they were related to each other and therefore to the Keller family, but for the life of me, I couldn't figure out how. I lay awake long after midnight trying to watch the pieces slide into place, but they just wouldn't.

Still, the next day, I had work to do. Santiago had given us the go-ahead to take down the O'Malley cabin, and Saul and his crew were ready to do the work. The house at the lot was basically finished, as far as they were concerned, so now it was my job to take over with decor and furniture. But that would have to wait until we finished the job that had started this whole fiasco.

Bright and early that morning, I dropped Sawyer off at school and headed up the mountain to the cabin. When I arrived, Saul and his team were already lifting off the roof. The rafters were in good shape, and I hoped that meant the rest of the logs would be, too. It would be a huge gift financially to be able to sell a full cabin to someone who wanted to rebuild it or use it for part of a larger build.

As we moved down the levels of the cabin, we found a few logs that had succumbed to rot or termites, and one wall was worse than the others because it had been on the north side of the cabin. By and large, though, we had an entire cabin disassembled by the end of the day, and I was fairly sure any logs we couldn't use could be replaced with ones we already had on the lot.

Saul drove the truck of logs down the mountain, and the rest of his crew followed with the other trucks and trailers loaded with the equipment from the job. I stayed up on the mountain to do my usual perusal of the ground to be sure that not only had we not missed anything worth salvaging but also that we left the site as pristine as possible.

I did my walk-around, didn't find anything that needed tending, and got into my car. But when I got out to the logging road, something pushed me to go up the hill instead of down. I wanted to see Katherine's campsite just one more time. I was still struggling mightily with my guilt over the fact that I hadn't been able to rescue her that day, and somehow, I thought seeing her campsite might help me.

My Outback was really good on rough roads, and since I'd been up and down this one a few times now, I knew it was wide enough to accommodate her. Still, I took it slow, not wanting to drop a tire into a deep hole that my girl couldn't get us out of. I kept looking around as I drove, hoping I'd see something that we'd all missed. But nothing stood out, no big neon signs that said, "Paisley Sutton, look here and you will find the missing woman."

By the time I got to the campsite, I was pretty discouraged with myself and the entire situation. Despite a great day on the jobsite, I was still haunted by the image of Paul Fletcher's body and the smoke of Katherine's campfire. I parked my car and took a walk around the tents and tarps again.

Like Santiago said, most of the personal effects had been taken by her parents. I stared for a long time at the little trash can that sat near Katherine's cot. I couldn't believe her parents would take her trash, too, but then, maybe they thought she'd implicate them in some crime. Who knew what people that horrible thought? If they could beat up a little girl, I supposed they were capable of anything.

Out of frustration, I pushed a few of the remaining items – the cot, a milk crate, a little table – around with my foot. I was being a bit like Sawyer when he lost his temper, but at least I wasn't modeling bad behavior. When I tipped over a wooden apple crate that Katherine had obviously been using as a bedside table, a tumble of photographs poured out.

I bent over and gathered up the photos. Right on top, in black and white, was Paul Fletcher standing right outside the cabin Saul and I had just completely dismantled. I flipped through more images – all of him around the cabin. Apparently he had been spending time there, which I thought was a little strange, but given how much the place had meant to him and Patrick O'Malley, maybe it wasn't that surprising. Goodness knew I'd been back to sentimental places that I'd shared with exes when I was in a low mood.

The stack of images was a couple inches thick, so I started to just flip through them. I watched Paul Fletcher move around the outside of the cabin like he was one of those characters in a child's flip book. I was almost to the end of the stack when another figure entered the frame.

I moved back through the images, each one bringing the second person's face more and more into view. I stared hard at the image of Paul and Patrick O'Malley standing with their hands on each other's shoulders. The men had been meeting at the cabin again, and Patrick had neglected to mention that information. My heart started to race, and my mind wasn't far behind.

I took out my phone to call Santi, but just then, I heard the distinctive sound of a heavy footfall breaking a stick. Everything in me said to run, but I resisted. I stood no chance in a footrace through the woods. Instead, I sprinted for my car, jumped in, and locked the doors. I figured I could call Santi while I drove, and so I shouted for my phone to dial his number.

Then, I threw the car into reverse and quickly realized I could not, by any means, back down this bumpy road without getting stuck. I took a split second to look around and see if I could turn around, but there was no room for my SUV to make it. So I threw the transmission into drive and floored it just as I saw a large shadow jump out of the woods toward my passenger's side window.

My car bounced and lurched up the hill, and I thought I was going to make it until I got to the gate at the top. It was locked tight – I could see the chain wrapped around the post and the gate itself, and the padlock was firmly closed. I was trapped, and behind me, I could hear the distinctive sound of a UTV getting closer.

Once again, I briefly considered running, but I stood no chance on the Parkway on foot. And if I ran off into the woods, I'd be easily overtaken. I paused, took a deep breath, dropped the car into low gear and gunned her right into the gate.

I had been on enough construction sites by now to know that anyone who wanted a post to stay in the ground sank it into a couple feet of concrete, but I also knew my car had never failed me. So when she bounced off the gate like Sawyer on his trampoline, I backed up a few feet and rammed the gate again.

She still didn't move, but I could hear the UTV getting closer and my phone wasn't able to get enough signal to connect a call. I had to save myself. This time, I could see the UTV speeding up the trail behind when I looked in the backup camera, so I got bold and charged backward into the UTV. The smaller machine stopped short, and a large male figure bounced around the seat. But then, he jumped out and ran toward me.

I prayed that my car was up to the challenge and charged

toward the gate again. This time, the post tugged free from the ground, leaving me just enough room to squeeze around it on the right and leave my own white blazes on the tree. Then, I was up and flinging my car right onto the Parkway.

In my side mirror, I saw the UTV pull up onto the Parkway, but when another car came toward me on the other side of the road, the green machine backed up onto the logging road and didn't come back onto the asphalt. I picked up as much speed as I dared on the twisty road, and just about the time I got to the exit back down to Octonia, my call finally connected.

"It's Patrick O'Malley. At least, I think it was him," I said to Santi. "He just chased me off the mountain."

"Where are you?" Santi shouted.

"On 33, headed your way." I could hear the fear in my voice and tried to take a few deep breaths. "Station?"

"No, my house. We need to get you secure. I'll meet you there, and I'm calling your dad to pick up Sawyer and bring him over." He let out a long breath. "Are you okay?"

"Terrified, but yes, and my car might need a little body work."

IT TOOK ALL my concentration to keep my hands steady and focus on driving the few minutes to Santiago's house. When I reached his driveway and saw him waiting there for me, I started to shake so hard I couldn't even open the car door. Santi was there, though, getting me out and into the house, and when he had me settled onto the couch, he put me on the phone with Lucille, who was with Dad at Sawyer's school. They were on their way.

I was safe, and Sawyer was too, and now, I had to push through and explain to Santiago what I'd found. I just hoped that O'Malley hadn't gone back and found the photos. When

I'd heard the footfall, I'd just run. I wasn't even sure where the photos were, but I was sure I hadn't hidden them again.

Santiago sat down next to me, and I told him about stopping at Katherine's campsite when I left the cabin, about finding the photographs of Fletcher and O'Malley, and about how I hadn't been able to get a good look at my attacker's face on the mountain but that it was definitely a man, a big man.

"A man the size of Patrick O'Malley?" Santiago said.

Of course, I had already assumed that Patrick was my assailant, but now I couldn't be sure. And I knew that it would be harder for Santiago if I gave him more confidence in that fact than I felt. "I don't know. Definitely a man. Definitely a tall, broad-shouldered man. That is all I can tell you because I couldn't see any features and only got the sense of it being a male because of the way he moved. I'm sorry."

Santiago pulled me to his chest. "Gracious, Paisley. Don't apologize. You were being chased in the woods. You've done nothing wrong. I'm just glad you're okay."

I let myself rest in his arms until I heard the front door open and little footsteps running toward me. "Mommy, I got to leave school early. Boppy said we could have ice cream."

With a smile toward my dad and Lucille, I said, "I think Boppy had a great idea. Santi, can you oblige us?"

"Chocolate or chocolate chip mint, Little Man?" Santiago said with a wink at me.

"Chocolate, please," Saw said. "I'll help you get it."

The two of them wandered into the kitchen behind us, and Dad sat down next to me and pulled me into his chest. "Paisley, you are going to be the death of me," he said as he squeezed me.

Lucille sat across from me, and in hushed tones so I didn't scare Sawyer, I explained what had happened. "And you don't know who it was?" she said.

I shook my head. "I just wish I'd grabbed the photos before I ran." Again, I had failed Katherine Forester when I got scared.

Saw and Santi returned from the kitchen with five bowls of ice cream. "Mommy, can I have some apple juice in my blue cup?"

I looked at Santi, who nodded. He had apple juice. "Your blue cup is in the car. Maybe you can get it for me, Lucille?"

"Absolutely," she said as she stood up. "Be right back."

The ice cream tasted wonderful, even though I didn't have much appetite. I tried to put on a good face for Sawyer, but all I wanted to do was sleep. I was exhausted.

Lucille came back in with Saw's cup a few moments later, and as she passed me, she said, "Maybe these will help." She dropped a pile of something onto the couch beside me.

I looked down, and there were the photos from Katherine's tent. "What?!" I said as I picked up the images.

"They were on your passenger's seat," Lucille said as she came back in the room with Saw's apple juice. "You must have dropped them there when you got into the car."

I stared at the photos as if they had come from the sky like manna, which they kind of had, and then looked over at Santiago. "Well, there you go." Suddenly, everything felt really funny, and I started to giggle.

Sawyer looked at me and said, "Mom, what in the world are you doing?"

I shook my head because I couldn't get enough air to form words, and apparently, I looked pretty silly because Sawyer started laughing, too. Soon, he and I were snorting and holding our bellies, and trying to catch our breath. It was just the release I needed, and when we both calmed down, everyone around us was smiling and shaking their heads.

Dad said, "The two of you okay now?"

I looked at Sawyer, who looked at me and started giggling

again. I restrained myself and nodded to my father. "Yeah, yeah, I am."

"Okay, good," Dad said. "Let's go play ball out back, Saw-Guy."

Sawyer jumped up, pumped his fist, and said, "Yes!" Dad picked up the baseball gloves and wiffle ball he'd brought over with him and followed his grandson outside.

As soon as they were outside, Santiago picked up the photos and began to flip through them one by one. His face mirrored what I had felt as I looked at the same images earlier. He went from puzzled to intrigued to outright surprised when he got to the images that included Patrick O'Malley.

"It seems Patrick has a bit of a memory problem," I said when he set the stack aside and met my eyes.

"That's one possibility," he said.

"More like a lying problem," Lucille said as she skimmed the photos herself. "Katherine Forester took these?"

I shrugged. "I'm guessing so, since they were in her tent, but they were tucked under a crate. I'm guessing that's why her parents didn't take them."

Santiago nodded. "I did see a camera in her tent when we first looked. A pretty good one, if I recall. I'll have to ask Frank and Nancy if she took a lot of pictures." He glanced at the stack of pictures in Lucille's hands. "Unfortunately, those aren't really something we can use as evidence, given that you basically stole from a crime scene."

The air left my lungs. "Oh no. I'm so sorry. I didn't mean to take them. I was just so scared—"

"Pais, you don't need to apologize. This is good information to have, and we have other ways to pursue the direction those give us." He got up and sat next to me. "I'm just glad you're okay, and honestly, if you hadn't taken the photos, whoever chased you might have. Then, we'd have no leverage."

"Leverage?" I asked as I felt the exhaustion settle into my bones like lead.

"Well, we can't use the photos as evidence, but Patrick O'Malley doesn't need to know that." Santi winked at me and then stood up, took the blanket off the back of the couch, and draped it over my legs. "Baby Yoda, anyone?" he said as he picked up the remote.

I smiled. "Yes, please." I looked over at my stepmother. "Dad okay with Saw for a bit?"

"Are you kidding? Time with his grandson and a chance for his daughter to rest? He wouldn't have it any other way." She slid onto the couch next to me and shared my blanket. "Besides, I haven't seen Baby Yoda yet, and I'm eager to see what all the fuss is about."

Santi turned on *The Mandalorian* and then left us to the show while he, I assumed, did some policing from his home office.

I woke up to the sound of a knock on the door. A few seconds later, Mika came in the door with her arms piled high with takeout containers. Behind her, Saul followed with a cooler, and finally, Savannah came in carrying what looked like an enormous hat box. I stared at the parade of food for a minute while I came out of my impromptu-nap stupor, and then I looked at my watch. It was after six p.m. I had slept for more than two hours.

Given that I had been sitting with my head thrown back on the couch, I imagined I had not only been snoring but probably also drooling. I felt much better than I had earlier, I decided to take the minor embarrassment as a gift.

I extricated myself from the blanket and followed everyone to the kitchen, where Sawyer said, "Mom, you were snoring," and confirmed that I had indeed made an exhausted fool of myself. Still, the fact that he had let me sleep that long was testament to how much Santi and my parents had convinced him I needed the rest, and the fact that he'd actually let me rest showed he was really growing up. I was grateful.

At that moment, though, I was most grateful for the assortment of Chinese food that Mika had brought with her. I fell into line around Santi's peninsula and fixed myself a plate of cashew chicken, beef and broccoli, and two egg rolls. There weren't enough egg rolls for everyone to have two, but given that I'd almost died *and* almost totaled my car that day, I gave myself permission to be greedy. When Mika slipped her roll onto my plate as she sat down, I took that as confirmation that my selfishness was acceptable today.

Conversation around the table was light while we all ate and drank from the impressive assortment of beers and sodas Saul had contributed. But the highlight of the meal was definitely the massive Boston cream pie that Savannah brought out for dessert. It was four layers high and full of cream, but the best part was the dark chocolate ganache dripping down the sides. I had thought I was pretty full until that beauty made an appearance. Then, I decided I could make a bit of room.

"Brava," Lucille said as she sliced dessert. "Where did you get this masterpiece?"

"Oh, I made it," Savannah said as Lucille stopped cutting to stare at her. "I took some classes to be a pastry chef back in the day." Her cheeks flushed a deep red.

"The things we learn about our friends," Lucille said. "Well, I will need this recipe, if you're willing to share. And you have to tell me how you get your custard to stand up in this heat."

The two women took their plates into the living room and continued their culinary conversation while the rest of us stuffed our faces at the table. Sawyer, the king of leaving two-thirds of everything on his place, even ate his entire piece. It was delicious.

Someone must have explained to Sawyer that we were having a slumber party at Santi's house because when his bedtime rolled around, he led the way back to Santi's bedroom, where he climbed into the middle of my boyfriend's bed and said, "Guess you'll just have to tell me a story tonight, Mama?"

I grinned. "I guess I will, Love Bug. So do you want a story about a dragon or about a fairy?"

His choice for the night was a dragon, and after a long, winding tale about the dragon who had lost his spark, Sawyer rolled over and drifted off to sleep like he was at home in our own bed. I lay there watching him sleep for quite a while, but when it felt like I might drift off myself, I got out of bed and joined the other adults in the living room.

The conversation didn't come to a screeching halt when I walked in, but I could definitely smell the metaphorical burning brakes as I sat down. "Please, don't stop what you were discussing because I'm here. My ears were practically burning off back there." I smiled and tried to reassure everyone it was fine if they were talking about me. "If you weren't discussing the day I've had, I'd be worried that you didn't care."

Santi looked at Dad, who gave a slight nod and said, "We have a crazy idea, and before you ask, everyone here thinks it's both insane and necessary. So no need to worry about other people's feelings."

I took a deep breath. "Crazy but necessary. Got it. What's this idea?"

"We want you to go talk to Patrick O'Malley tomorrow. Confront him. Show him the pictures. See what he'll tell you," Savannah said as she winced slightly.

As I looked at each person in the room, I knew that they had already pushed and poked at all the weaknesses and dangers in this plan, and I also knew that I was far too tired to do that kind of analysis myself that night. "Okay. Tell me what we're doing."

Mika looked at Santi who looked at my dad and then at Saul. Then, as choreographed, they all shrugged and Santi said, "I'll wire you up in the morning. Then, you can take the pictures over to O'Malley's place and ask him about why he didn't tell us that he and Paul had met up."

I nodded. "Okay, and what am I trying to get him to confess to? Murdering Paul? Trying to kill me? What?"

"Anything. But the top priority is to figure out where Katherine Forester is," Savannah added.

I looked at her carefully. "She was kidnapped by Collins and Keller. We know that for sure." I was very confused.

"We do," Santi said. "But given the photos you found and the fact that the person who chased you really didn't want you near her campsite, we're betting Patrick O'Malley is somehow involved with her kidnapping, too."

"We just aren't sure how," Savannah said, "but maybe you can find out."

I sighed. "I can try." Suddenly, the heaviness of all this was pushing me down into deep exhaustion again. "Maybe someone can write a loose script for me. Right now, I need to go to bed." I stood up and almost toppled right back over.

"Good, you do that," Mika said as Santi got an arm around my waist and held me up. "We'll get the script ready, and I'll plan to go with you tomorrow. Moral support won't seem odd, right?"

"I like that idea," Saul said. "And the guys and I will help the police out keeping an eye on things at your house and here, Paisley-girl. You just rest."

"Thank you, everyone," I said with as much sincerity as my tired body could manage. See you in the morning."

As Santiago walked with me down the hall, I said, "I suppose everyone is staying overnight."

He smiled. "Of course. Your dad and Lucille will get the guest room. Mika and Savannah are sharing the sleeper sofa, and one of Saul's friends dropped off a camper in the driveway while you were napping today. You'll be surrounded by your people tonight, Pais."

"Thank you," I said as I stripped off my jeans and climbed into bed in my T-shirt. "Really."

"Of course," he whispered into my ear. "Anything for the woman I love."

I smiled at his words, and they were the last things I heard before sleep overtook me again.

The next morning, I woke up to a tiny hand under my chin, tickling me. I groaned and pretended to be asleep as I rolled over, then I threw my leg over my son and tickled him until he shouted for me to stop.

Santiago was already up, and from the kitchen I heard the sound of the coffee grinder. I couldn't quite make out the scent, but the whole house smelled delicious. Apparently, Saw thought so, too, because before I could suggest it, he was out the door and down the hall to the kitchen.

I got myself up and wandered down in a pair of Santiago's boxers and my T-shirt. Savannah was just rising, too, but she had somehow managed to have a very cute set of pjs to sleep in. I really had to get a go-bag and put it by the door for this kind of situation. Maybe I'd suggest Mika do the same since she was in a similar ensemble to mine, but instead of Santiago's boxers, she was in a pair of his sweatpants rolled up about eight inches. She looked adorable and slightly silly.

Dad and Lucille had taken to sleeping late in their retirement, but even they had been roused by the smell of whatever Santiago was making. I couldn't blame them. It smelled sweet and rich, and I could feel my stomach growling against my ribs.

As I entered, I watched Santiago pull a huge casserole dish out of the oven. It was covered in something that looked like cinnamon, and I thought it might be coffee cake for a minute. But then, the richness of baked eggs hit. "Is that baked French toast?" I said as I walked over to hug him.

"Trying a new recipe. You'll be honest?" he said as he kissed my cheek.

"Sure thing. Just give me some right now," I said as I turned to the cabinet and pulled out six mugs and a small plastic cup. As the coffee finished brewing, I poured coffee for all the adults in the room and got Sawyer a cup of milk.

He and my dad were racing the salt and pepper shakers up and down the table, so I refrained from setting the liquids there just yet. Instead, I got out the hand-thrown creamer-and-sugar set from their spot and added half-and-half to the creamer. Soon, all the grown-ups were sipping the most delicious dark coffee.

Sawyer had moved along to stacking all of Santi's coasters in various configurations in the living room, and a few moments later, Saul came in, freshly showered and whistling. "Good morning," he said in his gravelly voice. "Is that breakfast?"

"Yes, sir. Come and get it, everyone," Santi said as he set out plates next to the casserole on the counter.

Soon, we were all eating the most rich and sweet casserole, and I took a second helping while saying, "I think you could say this one is a success."

He smiled. "Good to know," he said. Then, his face grew serious. "Now, we need to make our plan."

I swallowed the last of my bread and then got up for another cup of coffee. When I sat back down, I said, "Okay, I'm ready."

Lucille grabbed the gloves and ball and ushered Sawyer out the back door with a quick nod at me. "We'll be out here and then head to the goat house when it's time," she said from the doorway. The "goat house" was Sawyer's name for the local Mennonite market, and he *loved* to go there.

"Thanks," I said. "I don't know what I'd do without you."

She waved my words away and headed out, glove already on hand.

"Okay, so I need to call Patrick?" I asked, figuring this was the only way this might happen. "I just ask to meet?" I took out my phone.

Santi nodded. "I'd bait him a little. Tell him you found something you need to ask him about. See if he gives anything away on the phone. Maybe we can avoid putting you in harm's way." He didn't sound particularly optimistic on this point, but I thought it was worth a shot.

I tapped in the number from a slip of paper that Savannah slid in front of me, and even though it was kind of early (before eight a.m.), Patrick answered on the first ring.

"Hi, Patrick. This is Paisley Sutton. I came to see you with Sheriff Shifflett a few days ago."

He acknowledged that he remembered me and then said, "What can I do for you?"

"Well, I've come into possession of some images that you might like to see. Any chance you and I can meet this morning?" I tried to affect a tone of casual seriousness, but I could feel the tremor of fear starting in my hands.

"Images? Of what?" he asked.

"Let's just say that they involve the subject of our discussion the other day." I didn't want to give too much away because I knew there was value in the element of surprise being kept for our in-person meeting, but I did have to get him to meet somehow.

"Um, okay," he said. "At the coffee shop downtown in a half hour?"

"See you there." I hung up and then told everyone what he said. "He did sound confused and totally in the dark about the pictures, but maybe he's a good actor."

Savannah shook her head. "No, that sounds strange to me. I mean, if he chased you yesterday, he probably would have assumed that's the reason for the meeting."

"I agree. We're missing something," Santi said.

"Maybe she shouldn't do this," Dad said to the police officers.

"*She* is right here, and she's doing it," I said with a roll of my eyes in Mika's direction. "I need to get dressed."

"Me, too," Mika said.

Within ten minutes, both of us were back in our clothes from the day before and in the living room. Under Savannah's direction, I slipped a tiny microphone under my shirt and clipped it to my bra strap before tucking the transmitter into my waistband at my lower back. We were ready.

The drive down Main Street was very short, so we let Santiago, Savannah, Dad, and Saul get a head start. Saul and Savannah were going to be in Mika's shop across the street so they could keep an eye on things from the front window, and Santiago and Dad were going to be in a car just up the road listening in.

Patrick was there when Mika and I walked in, and we decided, as we waited for our orders, that she'd sit nearby but at a different table so as not to freak him out. He did look really nervous as I approached, and I had to squash my tendency to ease his nerves by smiling at him. This was serious business, not a casual meeting.

"Thanks for coming, Patrick," I said as I sat down. "I wanted to give you a chance to explain before I talked with the sheriff."

I set the photos down on the table and watched as he picked them up.

His face first warmed into a smile, which I assumed was because of the affection he felt for Paul Fletcher, but as he got into the latter section of the stack, he frowned and then looked up at me. "I should have told you we met that day."

"Which day?" I said as neutrally as I could.

"The day he was killed. We met at the cabin, just to say hi, and I left after a few minutes." He took a deep breath. "I should have told you."

"Yes, you should have," I said. "Why did you meet?"

He shook his head. "I don't really know. We both realized it was a mistake as soon as I got there. I guess we hoped we might rekindle things, but too much had happened. We'd moved away from each other too far." He gazed past me for a minute, but then came back to the present moment "But I didn't kill him. I should have told you about our meeting, I know. I'm sure it's hard to believe me, but I didn't kill him."

"You need to tell the police," I said, fairly sure he was telling the truth but absolutely sure I couldn't make that call myself.

"I will," he said, "right away." He looked up at me from the photos again. "I really want to know who did this to Paul. He was such a good man." He stood up. "Do you know who took these pictures?"

I studied his face for a minute, trying to determine his motive for asking. I decided he was just curious and said, "A young woman who was camping just up the road from the cabin. A friend of your cousin Frank and his wife."

He nodded. "She has a good eye," he said. "I dabble a little myself. She's got a good sense of light and position."

I sighed. "I'll tell her when I see her," I said more optimistically than I felt. "Please do go to the police."

He looked out the window toward the station. "Actually, I see the sheriff walking right over there. I'll go catch him."

I smiled as he jogged off across the street. Santiago put on a properly surprised face as Patrick yelled his name. *Good move, Santi*, I thought.

Mika sat down across from me. "He didn't chase you yesterday," she said with certainty.

"Agreed. That man was grieving, not attacking. And he didn't seem to harbor any malice or suspicion of me. He didn't see me up there," I said.

"That's what I thought, too, but then who chased you?" She stared at me a moment too long. "You're not safe yet."

I sighed. "I guess not."

"I texted Savannah when it seemed Patrick was telling the truth, and she confirmed that Collins was still in custody. So it wasn't him, either." Mika drained the rest of her drink. "Let's go to my shop and see what we can come up with."

I nodded and then looked at my own empty mug. "It's almost ten. You head on over to open, and I'll grab another cup of coffee for each of us and some for Savannah, Dad, and Saul, too. See you all over there."

Mika nodded and headed out. I tucked the photos into the pocket of my jeans and then went to the counter and ordered five cappuccinos to go. Then, while the barista steamed the milk, I took a seat in the back of the café to relax for a few minutes before my brain started going fast. I closed my eyes and leaned back against the leather sofa, listening for my name to be called.

A moment later, someone sat down on the couch next to me. I opened my eyes, expecting to see my dad or Mika, come to keep me company. Instead, I was looking into the red face of Frank O'Malley. "Don't say anything," he said. "Just come with me."

"Frank," I said. "What's going on?"

"Come with me," he said and moved the pistol in his hand

out from the back of the couch just enough that I couldn't miss it. "Now."

I stood up and walked in front of him toward the front door. The barista gave me a look as she set the last of my drinks on the counter, and I tried to communicate with my eyes that I was in trouble. I couldn't tell if she understood me.

Frank kept a hand on my shoulder and turned me left out the door and up the sidewalk. "Get in," he said as he stopped me beside an older Chevy pickup.

I did as he said, and while I entertained the thought of trying to run as he jogged around the front of the car, I knew he could shoot me down before I got far. And given that it was now clear that he had killed Paul Fletcher by shooting him in the back, I didn't think my odds were good.

Instead, I sat still and waited for him to get in on the driver's side. "What were you doing up at Katherine's campsite yesterday?" he asked as he started the truck.

"Nothing, really. I was just looking around. I was just frustrated and wished I could help." I figured the truth wasn't going to cause me any more trouble than I was already in. "Why were you there?"

He shook his head. "I came up to see the work you'd done, be sure the whole cabin was gone, but when I saw you go up the hill instead of down, I followed you. Saw you nosing around in there." He turned his head to look at me for just a second. "Didn't find anything, did you?"

The photos in my back pocket jabbed into my butt, but I shook my head. "No. You cleaned it out well. Smart move to make Santiago think Katherine's parents did it, by the way."

"Despicable people like that deserve all the trouble they get." His voice was gruff, and he looked like he hadn't slept in days. "Besides, I couldn't have you all knowing it was me."

"Why did you kidnap her, though? She was special to you." I was still missing a key piece of all this, and I couldn't help but try to figure out what it was. Then it hit me. "She saw you with Paul Fletcher."

"Bright girl – both of you. Katherine just couldn't stop with that camera. She came down to take some last pictures of the cabin before you took it down, and she saw me putting Paul's body into the cabin." He sighed. "I couldn't have her telling anyone until she understood why."

I took a small gift of hope that maybe she was still alive if Frank believed he could explain his reasons to her. "And why did you kill him?" I asked, hoping that I'd be able to share this information with Santiago, not just get some answers before I died.

O'Malley turned the car down a small road north of Octonia near his farm. I knew this road since Sawyer and I came here often to swim in the wide open section of river that had a small beach.

We parked, and O'Malley came around and forced me out of the truck by pulling on my hair. "Get down there," he said and shoved me toward the river.

He made me sit down on a rock by the water's edge, and then he sat down across from me. "I'm sorry to have to do this again in my life, but apparently, people just can't be trusted to do a job and then let well enough alone."

I kicked myself for stopping at that campsite, for the second time in as many days, but it would do me no good to feel sorry for myself now. "What did Paul do?"

"It's what he didn't do that's the problem. He promised Nancy his kidney, and then he backed out of the deal, said his conscience got the better of him." Frank shook his head. "He thought it was going to work for him to go to UVA and tell them he'd be a living donor for her, but those doctors, they don't listen to us country people."

I stared at him for a moment. "Frank, that *is* how it works." I'd done some reading on organ donation in the past few days, and I had made sure I was registered as an organ donor, but also looked up what I could do if someone I loved needed help. It really was a simple process of being tested and then directing the hospital to donate the organ to the recipient you intended. "Paul could have just said he wanted his kidney to go to Nancy."

For a split second, Frank looked like he was going to pass out, but then anger suppressed any sense of shock. "Poppycock," he said. "No fancy city hospital has ever done anything for us. We had it all worked out. Nancy was going to be fine, and Paul was going to get a nice payout. But he had to get it all by the book."

"So you killed him?" I said, wanting to be sure I heard the whole story but also hoping I could stall and figure out some escape plan for myself. With that gun pointed at my chest, though, I was having a hard time strategizing.

"Shot him right in the kidney. Fair penance, I figured." Frank's face had taken on a sort of sinister placidity. "He wasn't going to need either of them after that."

I winced at the sheer menace in his voice. "You shot him in the back intentionally, not because he was running away or something."

The smile that played across Frank's face chilled my blood. "I think that's what they call poetic justice."

Clearly, Frank O'Malley was proud of his actions, and that scared me more than anything. "Does Nancy know?"

"No. Of course not. She's innocent of everything. She would never take action like this. She's willing to die, if necessary, even with Lloyd Keller offering her a great deal since she was his kids' teacher." He shook his head. "But I can't lose her. Lloyd will figure out something."

A deeper chill sank into my bones, and I had to bite my tongue to keep from pointing out that Lloyd Keller was in no position to negotiate anything. "I'm so sorry about Nancy," I said, and I meant it.

For a second, he met my eyes and nodded. "Thank you, and I'm sorry for this, too. Really I am. But you were getting too close. I couldn't have you figuring things out. I would have made this a little more private up in the woods yesterday, but then you did that stunt thing with the gate."

I took a deep breath. "Frank, you don't have to do this. No one knows about our conversation, so you can just let me go. I'll even walk home from here. You can trust me."

A dark shadow fell over Frank O'Malley's face. "That's exactly what Fletcher said." He stood up then and turned me toward the river. "You won't feel it. I'll make it quick," he said.

I braced myself, even as I scanned for a rock I could grab and use to knock him out. I knew that was futile, though. I'd be dead before I could bend down. Tears pricked my eyes as I thought of Sawyer, and I said a small prayer of gratitude that Dad, Lucille, Mika, and Santiago would take care of him.

But then, I heard the sound of tires on the gravel behind me, and when I spun around, Santiago was leaping out of the car, his gun drawn. And Frank O'Malley had already put his hands over his head. It was over.

Dad raced over to me and pulled me to him just as I felt my knees give way. Savannah pulled in next, and I watched over Dad's shoulder as she and Santiago secured Frank and put him in the back of her cruiser.

I sank onto the beach and started to sob.

With Frank and the Kellers under arrest, I wasn't in any further danger, so Santiago drove me back to my house and asked Lucille to bring Sawyer over from his place ASAP. He fixed me a cup of tea, and Mika fussed around making sure I had a blanket and pillow, the remote close at hand, and a full delivery of groceries via Mrs. Stephenson, who closed the store for the afternoon to help.

Soon, Lucille and Sawyer were home, and Dad had returned from the walk he took through the woods behind the farmhouse to blow off steam. I'd noticed he had a hatchet in his hand as he walked off, and I imagined there were some small trees that had taken the brunt of his anger and fear.

Savannah was at the station handling the situation with Frank, and Santiago had taken the rest of the day to sit with me. I had felt such relief when I saw him jump out of the car that I hadn't even thought about how he'd found me. But after I got settled in, he asked Mika to help me take off the wire so that he could have Savannah check it over and log the recording of my conversation with Frank as evidence.

"You recorded that whole thing?" I said when I was de-bugged. "I didn't know it had that kind of range."

"It doesn't," he said as he looked over at my father. "But your dad was still listening just in case, when Frank approached you, and when he saw Frank lead you into his truck, he followed behind in my cruiser. I'm glad I left the keys with him after I went to talk to Patrick."

"My dad tailed us?"

"Yep, and he did a good job of not being seen. He called me and kept me abreast of everything, and I was right behind him. I'd been parked out by the road for about five minutes, and you were handling things so well that we just stood at the ready so we could intervene when necessary." He leaned over and hugged me. "I'm sorry to put you through that."

A small part of me was absolutely furious that he didn't rescue me, but the larger part that wasn't still terrified – and was also very relieved that we'd caught the killer – understood completely. I would have done the same thing, I expected. I couldn't reconcile those parts of myself at the moment, so I just nodded. There'd be time to talk more about that later.

"What about Katherine?" I asked. The young woman had been on my mind ever since Frank and I had talked about her.

But even in my fear, I'd been wise enough to not mention her. Frank spoke like he hadn't killed her, but I didn't want to encourage him to think of that as a possibility if he hadn't already.

"Nancy found her in the shed in their backyard today," Santi said. Then, after looking at my stricken face, added, "She's fine. Scared. Dehydrated and tired. But fine. Frank didn't harm her."

"Thank God," I said. "She's lucky he didn't kill her, too." That look of hatred on Frank's face wasn't one I would forget easily.

"Yeah, I'm guessing that since she only saw Frank leave Fletcher's body, he didn't think of her as an imminent threat." Santi shook his head. "He definitely sounded like he cared about her when we talked to him that first day, too."

I nodded. He had sounded that way, and I expected he did still care for her on some level. But his love for Nancy and his all-consuming desire to keep her alive dwarfed every other emotion at that point.

"And how is Nancy?" I asked. I couldn't imagine how she was feeling. She was already dealing with a terminal illness, and now she'd just found out her husband was both a kidnapper and a murderer.

"Devastated. Furious. Totally baffled," Santi said. "She had no idea that Frank had tried to broker a deal for a kidney on her behalf, and that alone would have been enough to knock the feet out from under anyone."

"But then he killed someone and kidnapped the woman she thought of as a daughter," Mika said. "Poor woman."

"Her fellow teachers have rallied around her, and she'll have good support. They've also started an organ donor campaign to see if someone in the area might be a live donor match for her." Santi leaned back and looked at the ceiling. "I hope they find someone."

I did, too, and I made a mental note to find out how I could support the campaign. As a single parent – one who had almost died that day – I couldn't take the risk to donate, myself, even if I was a match, but I could certainly help gather registrants. And I would, as soon as I had the strength to do more than sit still.

Now, though, I just wanted to be with my people, to rest, to enjoy the safety of my farmhouse. Sawyer climbed up in my lap and snuggled close. Soon, both of us were asleep, and when I woke in the middle of the night to find him curled against me under a blanket on the couch, I didn't even try to move.

OVER THE NEXT FEW WEEKS, all of the Kellers, Michael Collins, and Frank O'Malley were arraigned on their respective charges, and according to the district attorney, she wasn't going to have any trouble at all making a case to put each of them in prison for a long time. I couldn't say I was sad about that news, but it seemed a real tragedy that Frank O'Malley would spend the rest of his life, and maybe the rest of his wife's life, in jail, all because he made some terrible choices to keep her with him.

In positive news, a young woman from Harrisonburg turned out to be a match for Nancy O'Malley, and she was scheduled to give Nancy one of her kidneys before the end of the year. That was a big shiny silver lining for a really terrible chapter in our county history.

A few weeks after Frank O'Malley nearly killed me, Santi and I were enjoying the sound of the peepers on my porch after Sawyer was in bed. He'd officially accepted an offer on his place, and he was slowly but surely moving in. We were trying to figure out how to combine our two households into my one small house, and it was becoming clear we were going to need an addition. But that would have to wait until we had the funds to add a third bedroom and bath.

As we stared at the stars off the front porch, we talked about the raccoon that Santi had needed to extricate from a woman's kitchen after she let it in the night before. She hadn't had her glasses on when she called her cat in for the night, and this masked bandit had taken advantage of the comfy couch and the pantry full of goodies while she slept.

I then shared the story of the crystal doorknob lady who had decided she wanted me to be her source for all her salvaged hardware and was talking about incorporating some of Dad's woodworking in her designs. In the past couple of weeks since the new offices and store had been open at Saul's lot, my business had grown on both the retail and the salvage side. I felt confident that the addition on our house would be feasible by the end of the year if things kept up at this rate.

As ten o'clock approached, I felt my eyes growing heavy, and I was just about to stand up and say I was headed to bed when I looked over to see Santi down on one knee in front of me, a simple black box in his hand.

"I have no big gestures to show you, Paisley Sutton. No extravagant dinner or even a practiced speech. But I cannot wait another day to ask you if you will be my wife. Will you?" His voice shook as he spoke.

I stared at him for less than a second, and then I nodded and bent down to kiss him. "I can't wait to be your wife," I said. "We are going to get into so much trouble."

"You know it," he said. "Let's go tell Sawyer."

"Let's wait till morning. He's all tucked in already." I grabbed his hand and pulled him inside. We had big adventures ahead, and I could not wait another day to start them.

Read the next of Paisley's adventures in *Fatal Floss* - https://books2read.com/fatalfloss.

BECOME AN ORGAN DONOR

I am a registered organ donor, and I hope you will consider registering as well. The process is simple and free, and you could be saving a life or a number of lives.

Learn more and register here:
https://www.organdonor.gov/

Thanks for considering it. – Andi

A FREE COZY SET IN SAN FRANCISCO

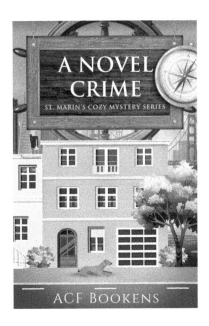

Join my Cozy Up email group for weekly book recs & a FREE copy of *A Novel Crime*, the prequel to the St. Marin's Cozy Mystery Series.
Sign up here - https://bookens.andilit.com/CozyUp

ALSO BY ACF BOOKENS

St. Marin's Cozy Mystery Series

Publishable By Death

Entitled To Kill

Bound To Execute

Plotted For Murder

Tome To Tomb

Scripted To Slay

Proof Of Death

Epilogue of An Epitaph

Hardcover Homicide

Picture Book Peril

Stitches In Crime Series

Crossed By Death

Bobbins and Bodies

Hanged By A Thread

Counted Corpse

Stitch X For Murder

Sewn At The Crime

Blood And Back Stitches

Fatal Floss

Strangled Skein

Aida Time

Poe Baxter Books Series

Fatalities And Folios

Massacre And Margins

Butchery And Bindings

Monograph and Murder - Coming in February 2023

Spines and Slaughter - Coming in April 2023

ABOUT THE AUTHOR

ACF Bookens lives in Virginia's Southwestern Mountains with her young son, old hound, and a bully mix who has already eaten two couches. When she's not writing, she cross-stitches, watches YA fantasy shows, and grows massive quantities of cucumbers. Find her at acfbookens.com.

Printed in the USA
CPSIA information can be obtained
at www.ICGtesting.com
LVHW020809150924
791100LV00037B/1242

9 781952 430411